TALES OF THE
GREATCOATS

SWASHBUCKLING FANTASY STORIES

SEBASTIEN de CASTELL

Dashing Blades
Books

The Eastern Desert

Duchy of
Pulnam

The Arch

hy of
rvor

Phan

Monastery
of Gazia

hy of
naris

The Bow

mor
of Kings"

Tristia

CONTENTS

PREFACE

There's a scene in Tyrant's Throne, the fourth and final book in the Greatcoats Quartet, when an enemy general tries to humiliate both Falcio and those foolish enough to follow him. This general argues – persuasively, I might add, that the true origins of the King's Travelling Magistrates come not out of some mythical past, but instead emerge from Falcio's shame over his failure to protect the woman he loved.

It's one of my favourite scenes because the very trauma the antagonist tries to use against Falcio is precisely what makes him so vital to the times in which he lives: he's someone who took his pain, his loss and his guilt, and turned those into a force for justice the likes of which even he could never have envisioned.

For all the sword fights and swashbuckling, the intrigues and grand political schemes, the Greatcoats Quartet is in many ways the story of one broken man trying to make sense of a world where his ideals seem to fail at every turn. It's Falcio val Mond's story, and everyone else is just living in it.

That, dear reader, is why this first volume of Tales of the Greatcoats exists.

There's so much about the King's Travelling Magistrates that excites and interests me, characters, places, and events I wanted to explore and that readers would ask me about, but to force those stories into the quartet would have violated the fundamental law governing that series: that this was Falcio's story.

Here then, are the stories those other Greatcoats. You'll meet Estevar Valejan Duerisi Borros, the King's Crucible. Part Hercule Poirot, part Mulder from the X-Files, upon whose broad shoulders (and, let's be honest, somewhat ample figure) falls the task of investigating incidents of the supernatural in Tristia. Almost from the moment he hit the page, I became enamoured of his intellect, his compassion, and perhaps most of all, his proclivity for pomposity. I decided early on that at least once in each story he would announce his full name to everyone around him.

You'll also travel with Murielle de Vierre, the King's Thorn, to the north of the country in search of answers and redemption. You'll follow in the footsteps of an assassin on the hunt for the greatest swashbuckler ever known, and stand beside a common wheelwright as she faces an impossible duel in the Court of Blades with only the strength of her heart and the counsel of a mysterious stranger.

Falcio himself makes an appearance or two, as does a

certain taciturn swordsman who hasn't stopped searching for justice in his own inimitable fashion.

Please be aware that all the stories in this book save one take place after the events of the Greatcoats Quartet. If you'd like to enjoy those books first, begin with Traitor's Blade, and from there pick up Knight's Shadow, Saint's Blood, and Tyrant's Throne.

As a final note, my gratitude to Peter Darbyshire, Kim Tough, and Lauren Campbell for their feedback and advice. I'm also indebted to Dr. Guy Windsor for making sure some of my bolder sword fighting tricks were actually possible.

Sebastien de Castell
Vancouver, Canada
November 4th , 2021

DEATH OF THE SWASHBUCKLER

A TALE OF THE GREATCOATS

SEBASTIEN de CASTELL

THE HUNT BEGINS . . .

Among assassins there is one target prized above all:
Falcio val Mond. But how do you kill the legendary Greatcoat reputed to have survived a hundred battles and once
duelled a god? Gavelle Sanprier believes he's found a way
. . .

AN EXCELLENT TIME FOR A MURDER

The assassination was to take place at the fourth bell after midnight. An excellent time for a murder, for the taverns had already cleared out, the city constables had started sneaking sips of throat-burning liquor from silver flasks secreted on their person to keep out the cold and wet, and with dawn coming so soon, even the wariest of victims might fool himself into believing that he was safe for the night.

And make no mistake about it: Falcio val Mond was a wary individual.

Gavalle Sanprier ended his third perambulation of the abandoned library's exterior, giving the dying building a brief salute before slipping inside. Even in its decline, there was something darkly beautiful about the decrepit old building. Three stories rose up from a sagging sidewalk that years ago had begun to dip into the canal waters. The City Masters had deemed the cost of restoration too great, and libraries – even the beautiful ones – unworthy of such vast expense.

Still, though, the decision can't have been easy.

The sweeping arches of the arcade fronting the ground floor conjured images of a better time, when artists and scholars might sit in the shade beneath those arches while painting their masterpieces or debating the finer points of philosophy, the latter no doubt periodically racing inside to find just the right book with which to score an intellectual victory over their opponents. Now the arcade was four feet underwater. Gavalle, garbed in specially oiled night-black trousers and duelling vest to keep from becoming soaked himself and imperilling his movements when the moment of val Mond's death arrived, made slow, methodical progress so as not to slosh the muck too much and risk alerting his victim.

'Are you sure you're ready for this?' Lucinda, his agent in these matters had asked for the third time yesterday before Gavelle had finally signed his name to the contract. 'Killing a Greatcoat is no easy thing and this one—'

'This one is frailer than you think,' Gavelle had told her, tracing a finger down her naked back as they lazed the day away in her bedroom. Gavelle had tapped a fingernail between Lucinda's shoulder blades. 'He took a rapier blade here last year,' he said, then let his hand trail down and inch to the right. 'The spiked ball of a morning star nearly shattered the bone even beneath his greatcoat here.' His hand drifted down further. 'A stab wound almost reached his kidney and ended him for good during the war with Avares, or so I'm told.'

'Why are you telling me all this?' Lucinda asked sleepily. 'I'm the one who provided you with the intelligence the client gave us, remember?' She sounded annoyed at Gavelle's presumption, but when she turned her face towards his, her smile suggested she already knew where all this was leading.

'I've been contemplating where to put the blade that finally ends the legendary Falcio val Mond,' he said, 'for it seems to me all the obvious targets have been tried before.' His finger slid down past her buttocks and between her legs. 'Perhaps somewhere here?'

Lucinda laughed, so brightly that were his eyes closed he would've taken her for a woman of seventeen instead of nearly seventy. For an assassin's agent, she had a remarkably sunny disposition. She crossed her ankles and squeezed her thighs together – damn, but the woman had strong legs! – trapping his hand between them. 'There now, you see?' she asked tauntingly. 'You've fallen into my trap, my gullible young assassin. Who's to say the Greatcoat won't trick you the same way?'

Gavelle waited until she'd released his hand before bringing it up to his face and inhaling. 'Then I pray to the Good God Death that his arse smells as sweet as your nethers.'

Truth be told, Gavelle didn't like the smell of Lucinda's nethers all that much – or anyone else's, for that matter – but it seemed a romantic thing to say, and both his future prospects and his current ones relied on Lucinda's goodwill towards him.

The stench of the canal water brought him back to the

old library. His progress through the stinking ocean of rotted pages and moulding leather covers that floated along the surface was slow but silent.

Silence was his gift.

Despite the claims Lucinda sometimes made on his behalf during fee negotiations, Gavelle wasn't, in fact, a Dashini. But he'd spent nearly a decade researching their ways, consulting those few scholars who knew something of their habits, following the gruelling and soul-crushing regimen they recommended.

Patience – that was the key. The Dashini didn't simply study their target before killing them. They *moulded* themselves to their victims, uncovering every detail of their lives: every childhood accident might have left one knee infinitesimally less steady than the other; every duel won or lost; every flower whose scent they were reputed to find nauseating.

Thanks to the exhaustive research the client had provided them, Gavelle now knew Falcio val Mond better than his own wife did – better than the man himself, he reckoned. In a way, they were like brothers now, and this building like a childhood home to them both. Gavelle had memorized every inch of the ruined library, not merely from plans but by several reconnaissance missions prior to val Mond's arrival in the city. He could navigate all three floors blind, not merely knowing its halls and chambers, but every crack in the tiles of each floor, which ones could take his weight without making a sound, and which ones could not.

At last, he reached the stairs at the back of the waterlogged floor, felt inside his pockets for the very special collection of tools the client had provided to Lucinda, and she in turn to Gavelle, so that he could accomplish what no assassin, no Knight or Duke, no Saint nor even a God had ever been able to do: tonight, in exactly fourteen minutes, Gavelle Sanprier would kill Falcio val Mond.

Gavelle set off up the stairs, removing from his pocket a tiny piece of folded cheesecloth no larger than his thumb. He unwrapped it quickly and popped it into his mouth. The Greatcoats called it 'The Hard Candy', and the moment it touched his tongue his senses exploded around him. Even in the dim light afforded by the moon through the broken mortar of the galleries, it was now bright enough for him to see every detail of the second floor as he left the stairwell. The smell of the canal water, unpleasant before, was now almost painful to him. He didn't mind, though, for the way his muscles played beneath his black garments promised a speed and strength beyond that of normal men. The first time the client had procured a sample, Gavelle had thought himself transformed into a Saint. Now he better understood its workings, and would not be swayed to arrogance when the moment came to face val Mond.

He could smell him now from the reading chamber at the end of the hall. The client had spent what Gavelle expected was a small fortune to get word that the former First Cantor of the Greatcoats would be in the city tonight, seeking out an old duelling text among the rot and ruins, apparently.

I hope you've found your book, Gavelle thought as he

drew the narrow-bladed smallsword from its sheath, the unnatural length not especially suited to his reach, but a full inch longer than the rapiers Falcio wielded – another of the client's revelations. *Because someone wants you to die very badly tonight, my brother.*

2

ERRERA BOTTIO

Gavelle watched a moment from the doorway of the massive chamber, with its tall columns supporting a sagging roof, the once majestic plaster walls stripped of their former gilding, the marble ripped from the floors by a generation of thieves and vandals. Falcio val Mond sat on a chair missing one of its legs that creaked every time he leaned over the decaying wooden scholar's desk, holding up a reading glass to the smudged and rippling pages of a book that looked as if a stiff breeze would reduce it to a thousand fragments of rotten paper.

Even from this distance – nearly forty feet away – Gavelle's now-enhanced vision revealed to him every detail of Falcio val Mond's face. The man looked not so much old as used up. A handsome face, Gavelle supposed, to some. He felt an odd stab of jealousy then, as he wondered whether Lucinda might fancy this former Greatcoat more than her assassin lover. A strange and petty thought, but one that would be removed from consideration momentarily.

Gavelle had considered introducing himself. There was no need for subterfuge, after all. The client's instructions had been specific and direct: he must die by the sword, his life and dignity stripped from him one piece at a time using the very same tricks and tools that have kept him alive until now.

Lucinda had shown Gavelle the client's note. The writing had been crisp and plain, and yet to Gavelle's eye, there was a barely restrained hatred beneath those scrawled lines of ink, a cold and calculated fury. How much did you have to hate a man to put this much thought into his death?

Gavelle was about to speak when the chair's three legs screeched along the floor as Falcio rose from his desk. Gavelle watched as the man tilted his head left and then right – a habit he was known for prior to a duel – and began buttoning up his coat.

'You heard me coming? Gavelle asked.

Still facing away from him, Falcio val Mond shook his head.

'You were silent as the grave.'

Gavelle brought the point of his smallsword up into guard. 'You knew I was coming?'

Falcio turned and drew the twin rapiers scabbarded to the sides of his long leather coat. 'Someone's always coming. Had it not been you, it would've been someone else.'

So much weariness, Gavelle thought. *You'd almost think he wants me to kill him.*

Gavelle was conscious of the time passing. The formulation of the hard candy was a secret lost when the previous King's apothecaries left Tristia, and the square Gavelle had swallowed, potent as it was, lasted mere minutes. Roughly fourteen, to be exact. Yet, as the two men walked casually across the floor towards one another – no rushing or tense postures for experts like them – he found a question coming to his lips.

'The book,' Gavelle asked, nodding to the rotted text on the desk by the broken remnants of the windows. 'You came back to Rijou for that book?'

Falcio nodded.

'May I ask what it is?' Gavelle asked.

Falcio wetted his lips, probably realising it had been too long since he'd had something to drink or eat – another of his foibles the client had informed them about – and would now be fractionally slower in his lunge and parries.

'You know Errera Bottio?' Falcio asked.

'"For You Are Sure To Die"? The old duelling manual?'

'That's the one. You've read it?'

Gavelle shrugged. 'Once, years ago. I never found it all that insightful. Most of it is an examination of the seven types of duellists.'

'Eight.'

Gavelle thought back to his reading of the book. 'Are you sure? I would've sworn—'

'Almost every copy of the book details the tactics and strategies of seven categories of duellists,' Falcio explained. 'The Avertiere, Master of Feints. The Ludator,

Master of the Ground Game. The Vinceret, Master of the—'

Gavelle slid his smallsword into its scabbard only to unsheath it with what he felt was impressively blinding speed. 'Master of the Quick Draw.'

Falcio gave a curt nod, his eyes not leaving Gavelle's, acknowledging his opponent's superior talent and technique. 'There were rumours that Bottio's original text named an eighth category of duellist. The Delusor.'

Gavelle chewed on the archaic word a moment. 'The "Illusionist"?'

'The translation is tricky. "Delusor" means Master of Deception, but the conjugation implies the past tense. The strategy of the Delusor is to connive to induce trifling wounds and injuries to his opponent days, sometimes weeks ahead of the fight. Thus when the duel begins . . .'

'The battle has already been lost.' Gavelle smiled – this, too, was a well-known tactic of the former First Cantor of the Greatcoats. He wiggled the point of his smallsword in the air reprovingly. 'You seek to make me doubt myself. You want me to wonder if somehow this was all a set-up, that somewhere around this building your confederates lie in wait so they can rush out and kill me before my blade reaches your heart. But you've been outwitted this time, Falcio. My associate has had men watching the library day and night for over a week. You are all alone, I'm afraid.'

'All alone,' Falcio agreed. He gestured with his left-hand rapier to the emptiness around them. 'Tonight's black deeds will transpire only between the two of us, Gavelle. You have my word as a Greatcoat on that.'

'I don't need your word,' Gavelle replied, irritated at the man's insinuation that he needed any such assurances. Bringing his point up into line, he began a slow, perambulating spiral inside the great reading room – one practiced a thousand times, designed specifically to work against Falcio's habits and reflexes. Anticipation for the kill buzzed like fireflies in his veins. This! Right here! A moment for the ages! From this day forward, Gavelle Sanprier would become the most famous and sought-out assassin in the entire country.

So why did the tired, aging Greatcoat slowly matching his movements seem so unafraid – not so much as resigned as ... bored?

'Wait!' Gavelle said, just as the two of them had come into measure with each other and their blades met in the centre. 'How did you know my name?'

3

THE DELUSOR

G avelle dove underneath val Mond's lunge, coming up on the Greatcoat's right flank and driving the sharpened quillion of his smallsword's guard into his side. The point tore through the leather and lining only to smash against the slender yet infamously durable bone plate sewn within.

Gavelle grinned. These duelling magistrates relied too much on their coats for protection, and regardless of how val Mond had learned about his coming, Gavelle knew something very important about Falcio as well: the location of a previously cracked plate in the front of his coat.

Let's play a while, you and I, he thought, shoving the off-balance Falcio away as he prepared his next attack. *But I know the exact inch of your body where my blade will end you.*

'Was it Lucinda who betrayed me?' Gavelle asked.

Falcio already appeared shaken. Tired. When he had to move, he did so with fierce speed, but in between, he slowed, conserving his strength.

'Do you love her?' Falcio asked.

Gavelle found the question unseemly, and punished his opponent with a flurry of thrusts from the high inside line to the lower outside line, ending with a slash that would've taken out the Greatcoat's left eye had he not fallen back.

'Love is an awkward pastime for an assassin,' Gavelle said, pretending to give Falcio time to recover even as he reached behind his back for the hidden pocket in his night-black duelling vest that hid a small satchel of blue powder. Another of the client's gifts.

Falcio smiled at him, and what was most strange about that smile was that it appeared genuine. 'An awkward pastime for many of us, my friend.'

'Ah,' Gavelle said as he secreted the powder in the palm of his rear hand. 'You speak of your wife. Is it true that she's the new Saint of Mercy?'

Falcio's grin turned rueful. 'She's not particularly merciful with me.'

A Saint. Now those could be trouble. If rumours were true, their mystical awe could bring even the most willful of men and women to their knees.

'A pity she's a hundred miles from here,' Gavelle said. 'I paid a few silver from my fee to ensure that fact before coming. I didn't want you to have to die in front of her eyes.'

'My gratitude,' Falcio said.

Their blades engaged at the sharpest and weakest points. Gavelle's was the lighter weapon, and Falcio attempted to use his blade's greater weight to gain leverage in an envelopment nearly sent the smallsword flying from Gavelle's hand.

'Damn, but you're good,' he muttered.

Falcio gave another curt nod, but didn't reply. There was a glistening on the skin of his forehead, and his mouth was open.

He's breathing hard, Gavelle thought. *Just as the client predicted!*

First, a feint with the point of his smallsword – a thrust above the eye that forced val Mond to duck. Next, Gavelle flung out his rear hand, sending the glittering flecks of blue powder right into his opponent's face at the exact moment he gasped for breath. When Falcio val Mond stood up again, swinging his rapier wildly to keep his foe at bay, his face was a mask of terror.

'Dashini dust,' Gavelle explained. 'I'm told you've trained yourself to be resistant to it, as much as anyone can at any rate. Alas, my aim isn't to disable you, merely to weaken you piece by piece.'

Falcio's mouth was working, mumbling like an old codger haunted by nightmares.

'Tell me,' Gavelle said eagerly. 'What do you see? What terrors does the dust bring upon you? Your new wife murdered in the same fashion as your first? The child inside her slain before it can be born? Perhaps your comrades in the Greatcoats, Kest and Brasti, hunted down and murdered in ways that will make your own soul shriek from beyond the grave?'

Falcio shook his head, but the effects of the toxin wouldn't be so easily dismissed. Gavelle circled the confused, frightened man, the tip of his smallsword evading Falcio's blade easily, delivering shallow cuts to his hands, his face, his neck.

'You fought a Sanguinist once,' Gavelle said. 'Bottio claims it's the worst way to die – a hundred tiny cuts bleeding you out drop by drop until you're begging for a more merciful death. Is that what you desire from me now, Falcio? A quick end? Come, you're the finest – well, the *second*-finest now – duellist the country's ever known. Call me brother and ask me for the final blessing of my blade.'

At first, the Greatcoat was silent, trying a dozen different manoeuvres to create distance between himself and Gavelle, but at every turn he failed, all the while shaking his head, growling like an animal as he fought to stave off the fear slithering inside his heart.

I'll soon kill that snake for you, Gavelle thought.

Through gritted teeth, the Greatcoat asked. 'Do you even know why you're doing this? Why someone would pay you a fortune to kill a retired Greatcooat?'

Gavelle had asked Lucinda the same question, two months ago when the contract had first come.

'You've made too many enemies, brother. Foiled too many ambitions. There is a line of powerful men and women a mile long who wish to see you humiliated like this, taken apart one precious piece of your soul at a time, and finally put down like a dog. As to why *I* was chosen? It is because I'm the best there is, Falcio.'

Gavelle saw an opening and swung the flat of his smallsword against val Mond's exposed left knee. The

Greatcoat went down with a scream that filled the entire reading hall.

'It was inevitable, if you think about it,' Gavelle went on, circling him. The effects of the hard candy were dissipating now, and his own muscles complained from the exertions he'd put them through, but he was still more than fast enough to make the kill, and far less injured than his prey. 'You should've known someone would seek out the greatest living master of the art of death and send him to you.'

Falcio tried to rise, failed, and landed hard on his knees, his rapiers clattering against the ruined library floor. He cried out again as he forced himself upright. There was courage in this man or belligerence at the least. He wanted to face his enemy as he died.

'Call me brother,' Gavelle urged. 'And let's make an end of it.'

'Brother . . .' Falcio murmured, his eyes barely open now. Gavelle had to reach out and grab him by the jaw to force him to meet his gaze even as he placed the tip of his smallsword against the spot on his Greatcoat. The one the client had informed them was already broken. The one through which steel would pierce flesh, slip between ribs, and kiss the heart of the legendary Falcio val Mond.

'Call me brother again,' Gavelle commanded. 'I like the sound of it.'

Falcio looked up at him, panting from pain and exhaustion. 'You know, I really thought I was better than this. I thought . . .'

'You thought you were still the best. But you couldn't be, you understand that, don't you, Falcio? No duellist can fight so many battles, incur so many injuries over the years, without weakening.'

He nodded, and his empty hand gestured back to the reading desk. 'That's why I'd been thinking about old Errera Bottio and his depressing duelling manual.'

Gavelle glanced over at the rotting book. 'The Delusor. The Eighth Duellist. The one who masters deception to defeat his opponent before the fight has begun. Too bad you waited too long to find the book.'

'Oh, I found it months ago,' Falcio said. 'Shortly after my wife informed me we were to have a baby. It occurred to me that eventually, someone was going to send whoever the latest and greatest murderer for hire might be after me.'

Gavelle had been about to thrust his blade through the flaw in the coat and into the man's heart. 'Too bad you waited too long to find the book' had seemed an excellent line on which to memorialize his victory. But his sword arm hadn't moved, and he found himself staring into the too-calm eyes of his victim.

Falcio nodded, sweat-soaked hair pasting itself over his forehead. 'As you said, it was inevitable. And sure, I might beat one or two assassins, but eventually, I'd find someone like yourself – someone too good for me.'

Gavelle leaned back and pressed the tip of his smallsword a fraction deeper against the flaw in Falcio's coat. 'Someone who knew all your weaknesses.'

'Exactly. Funny thing about that. How exactly did you learn all these details about me.' Before Gavelle could answer, the Greatcoat raised a finger. 'Ah, the client, right? This mysterious benefactor who gave you Dashini dust and hard candy and the location on my coat where the damned bone plate split a while back.'

Suddenly aware that something was very wrong, Gavelle drove the tip of his smallsword into the weakened spot . . . only to have the point meet impenetrable resistance. Before he could withdraw and make a second attempt, Falcio's hand flung out, and suddenly Gavelle's face was immersed in dust. He tried to step back, but his limbs betrayed him, unmoving, leaving him teetering like an old pillar by the canal waiting to fall in the waters at last.

'Aeltheca,' Falcio said, grimacing as he rose to his feet. 'Foul stuff. Paralyzes you for an hour or so. You should've gone with that instead of the Dashini dust. But I guess I forgot about it when I was drawing up the assassination contract.'

Of course, Gavelle thought, his mind whirling as he sought out the means to turn the tables back in his favour. His eyes could still move a little, and he gazed out at the reading chamber in this abandoned library. The perfect place to mount an assassination, but even more so if your desire is to ensure no one else can interfere with a ruse. *That's how he knew my name. Lucinda never betrayed me! Falcio val Mond is the client!*

Gavelle tried to speak, first to curse this man who'd tricked him so dishonourably, than to attempt a negotiation.

He never kills a fallen foe, Gavelle told himself. *It's not his way.*

But then Falcio val Mond put a hand on his shoulder,

not in anger or to push him over, but almost as a comrade might. A brother.

'I'm sorry,' he said. 'If I were younger, if I were as good at duelling as people believe, I could afford to have arse-holes like you come after me at their leisure. But I have a wife now, and soon – assuming her supposed "Saintly insight" isn't just a load of bollocks – a daughter.'

He sighed, and looked almost lost for a moment.

'I need them to fear me, Gavelle. All these Lords and Viscounts with their petty plots of revenge. I need them to . . . to be in awe of me, so they won't try this again.'

Again he patted Gavelle's shoulder, though Gavelle was having trouble feeling it now.

'The hard candy you took. I had it mixed with a portion of what we call the "soft candy". It's what we used to carry so that if we were in danger of torture, we might have a gentler, kinder death. The apothecaries promised the passage would actually be quite pleasant.'

No, Gavelle thought, raging against the effects of the aeltheca powder and the damnable poison he'd willingly ingested. *Such ends are for feeble, aging fools like yourself, Falcio, not men of pure will . . .*

He set his resolve against the paralysis, commanded idle muscles to contract. It was like trying to push through stone.

It can't end like this, he swore silently to himself, to the Gods, but most of all, to thrice-damned Falcio val Mond. Then, almost at the moment he was ready to give up, the fingers of his right hand twitched. *Of course!* he realized, exulting in the feeling of his fingertips returning. *The fool measured the dosage for himself, but he's older than I am, weaker. The would-be Delusor has unwittingly tricked himself!*

With a single movement, smooth as silk against silk, Gavelle's hand reached into the cuff of Falcio's own coat where the Greatcoats were known to secret one-inch blades, found the weapon, removed it, and before val Mond even understood what was happening, drew a red smile across his throat.

'Good . . .' the man gurgled, and blood so bright it shone like liquid rubies as it began to pour from the wide gash in his neck. 'Good . . .'

'Oh, better than good,' Gavelle said, though for some reason he couldn't hear himself speak. Perhaps his tongue needed more time to awaken.

'Good . . .' Falcio repeated.

Why did he keep saying that over and over? Or had he only said it once? Was it, in fact, only the beginning of an utterance, caught in this single moment of time?

Something terrible happened then. Something that should have been impossible: the blood seemed to flow back up into Falcio's throat, and the fatal cut Gavelle had inflicted on him faded as if it had never been there.

No . . . he thought as the light in the reading hall began to fade and val Mond's words returned to him: '*The apothecaries promised the passage would actually be quite pleasant.*'

Gavelle felt himself drifting into another dream, this one in Lucinda's bed as he recounted his daring victory over the supposedly undefeatable Falcio val Mond, but he resisted. Even as life dripped out of him like the leaks in the library floor, he forced himself to witness the world as it was, not as his own lethal vanity had promised him it would be.

Falcio was still there. He was manoeuvring Gavelle's body towards the windows and the light from the stars shining down on the canal. Then the Greatcoat walked away, leaving Gavelle Sanprier to meet his end, the strained limp of the Greatcoat's footsteps stopping only briefly when he said, 'Goodbye, brother.'

THE END

A STUDY IN STEEL

A TALE OF THE GREATCOATS

SEBASTIEN de CASTELL

THE LESSON BEGINS . . .

Time and time again, sixteen-year-old Percevar has proven himself too craven and incompetent to wield a sword for the honour of his house. But when his half-sister Aline's life is threatened by the machinations of their unscrupulous relatives, Percevar must learn once and for all the lesson of the blade.

1

THE LANGUAGE OF SWORDS

The rapier blades clink like wine glasses when the duellists cross swords for the first time. There's no clanging or clattering, instead, I hear the opening note of an unbearably graceful tune, performed by two masters playing their instruments in perfect harmony. The freshly sharpened edges graze against one another like the fingertips of two dancers passing each other on the stage. Leather-soled boots glide across the marble floor, never stomping, never slipping. Every movement is precise. Assured. Calculated.

The noble families in their cushioned seats by the railings and the rabble clamouring from behind on rough, splintery benches grin and nod at each other, united for once by the perils and prestige meted out within the duelling circle. The spectators jeer and shout at those seated on the opposite side of the court, negotiating wagers with elaborate hand gestures, fingers darting back and forth as speedily as the thrusts and parries of the combatants. So aroused are the audience's passions that they've become blind to all but the flash of steel upon steel. Deafened by the cacophony of their own applause, their ears fail to follow the deadly conversation unfolding inside the duelling circle. This is more than violence; it is poetry, composed in a language that goes unrecognized by the cantankerous crowds of the Rijou's infamous Court of Blades.

I understand it, though. Every word, every whisper.

It makes me sick.

Like all proper young gentlemen of Rijou, I've devoted hundreds of sweating, tearful hours inside the fencing halls where the sons and daughters of our city's notable families train in the ways of the sword. Within those walls, my name has become synonymous with awkward, incompetent bladework. 'Percevar Tiarren!' our master will shout, and my fellow students will pause in their own bouts to roll their eyes at my latest gaffe. The admonishments have become so frequent this past year that now whenever one of my classmates stumbles into a failed lunge, their partner will hiss, 'Don't *percé* your attack, silly.'

I'd take offence at this misuse of my name, but doing so would inevitably lead to a duel with blunted foils at midnight, and I get enough bruises in the classroom as it is. As has been pointed out to me many times – often with the tip of the master's own sword – I am rubbish as a fencer. 'You've learned nothing from me!' he declares at the end of every lesson. 'Nothing!'

He's wrong, though. I've learned this language of steel. I just can't bear to speak it.

My father, Lord Tiarren is one of the most respected generals in the Ducal army and a highly regarded duellist. Last night he asked me – no, *begged* me, his own son – to accept the junior officer's commission he purchased for me and accompany him to quell the border raids. As the second eldest child, tradition dictates that I become our house champion when I turn of age. To me, it will fall to protect my parents as they age, my eldest sister as she leads our house, and my younger siblings as they expand our business ventures. It is for me to fight duels on behalf of our family.

When I refused my father's offer for the third time, he didn't hit me with one of those big, iron-hard fists of his; he didn't threaten to expel me from his house and have my name stricken from our family line. He merely nodded as if he'd known all along what my answer would be, and accepted it as the unfortunate but inevitable consequence of congenital cowardice.

But I'm not a coward. I'm *not*.

At least, I don't think I am. I'm just afraid all the time.

The duel inside the courtroom changes tenor, the rhythm accelerating, drawing my attention back to the fighting circle. The combatants' probing rapiers having uncovered any weaknesses in defence or stiffness of movement, the blades now slither like snakes against each other, searching for an opening. The defendant, Orlo Abradi is a former guard captain to one of the High Twelve houses, convicted of attempting to swap a near-priceless blue romantine gemstone meant for his employer's anniversary necklace with a mere sapphire.

Orlo is a tall man, broad in the chest and long in the arm. This gives him greater strength and reach than his opponent. When the duel began, the heralds dubbed him 'Our Lord of the Battering Blow'. Orlo is indeed a formidable figure who's probably never lost a fight in his life. The loud swish of his blade as he slashes at the prosecuting duellist and the grunt he makes a split-second before his lunges tells me that Orlo should've accepted the magistrate's sentence of seven years for his crime instead of appealing for trial by combat.

A *duella damnatio* is sometimes called a 'gambler's duel' because every cut the defendant scores against the prosecuting duellist strikes a year from his sentence. Every wound he suffers, however, extends his prison term by a year, and like all gamblers playing at the wrong table, Our Lord of the Battering Blow doesn't know when to fold on a bad hand.

'Sixteen!' The audience shouts in unison as the prosecutor's point slips under the defendant's guard to nick his sword arm uet again. Before Orlo can even react, the prosecutor ducks down low and extends his arm in a perfect thrust that drives the tip of a blackened steel rapier a half-inch into the defendant's right thigh. A tiny spot of blood blooms red against the white duelling breeches. 'Seventeen!' The crowd cheers, as if they were the ones who'd scored the touch.

When Orlo tries a mad rush in retaliation, the lithe, whip-quick prosecuting duellist casually sidesteps the attack, flicking a trickle of blood from the tip of his rapier as if he were already done with the duel. Bézan Réchambeau is both shorter and leaner than his opponent. Here in the Court of Blades, he's referred to as 'Our Lord of Midnight' by his admirers for the unusual ebony sheen of his rapier blades, and by his bigoted detractors for the colour of his skin. Bézan is a foreigner to our shores, a former slave, or so the minstrels claim in their songs about him. Tristia has never in its history tolerated slavery, yet when I witness Bézan fence, I'm overcome by the sense that he's as eager to turn his blade on the audience as his opponent.

With an agonized roar, Orlo Abradi begins a series of reckless slashes at Bézan's face. The inelegant and brutish maneuver earns him heckles and catcalls from the nobles in the galleries. 'Our Lord of the Blundering Blowhard!' someone below in the cheap seats shouts, and is rewarded with slaps on the back and the echo of this new epithet rippling through the crowd like a wave that crashes down on me, threatening to drown me.

The raw pleasure, the bloodlust in their eyes . . .

The vein in my neck begins to pulse with the cadence of every thrust and counter-thrust. My breath catches with each feint and evasion. My throat tightens uncontrollably whenever one of the opponents lunges. When the defender's parry comes at that last possible instant, I can feel the force of the blow rattling my own bones. Only my white-knuckled grip on the railing keeps me from fleeing the duelling court.

There is something deeply wrong with me.

'Strike into his lower left line!' the twelve-year-old girl

next to me cries out exuberantly. 'He's putting all his weight on his forward foot!'

My little sister's advice will never reach the ears of the duellists, of course, but today is Aline's birthday, so I don't bother telling her so. It's my birthday, too, as a matter of fact: the two of us were born on the same day, four years apart. Unlike me, however, Aline adores fencing above all things. So I keep my mouth shut and feign as much enthusiasm as I can. In return, she gazes up at me with those mischievous brown eyes of hers and grins, and that makes it easier to swallow the coppery taste on my tongue that's been there since the duella condamno began.

'Little girls who know not of what they speak ought to speak far less,' our aunt interjects, the sharpness of her tone is like a stiletto blade jabbed in my ear. Her gaze darts all around us, searching for any sign that one of the noble families in our section might be frowning at Aline's commentary. Lady Valoise Porvos, slender-but-not-too-slender, tall-but-not-too-tall, and above all, sensual-but-never-wanton in both manner and dress, has an uncanny eye for disapproval. The other eye she reserves for intrigue. 'The Margravina Leandre has kept her bosom turned away from that foul little husband of hers throughout the entire trial. And see there how her hand touched the arm of her servant? There is something there, I think . . .' My aunt pauses to remove a tiny notebook from the cuff of the sleeve of her ruffled crimson trial gown. Here in Rijou we have fashions for everything, and besides, the red tiretaine cloth hides the occasional splatter of blood.

'That big, dumb brute will never score against Our

Lord of Midnight if he keeps swinging his blade so wide-ly,' my little sister admonishes. Bézan Réchambeau is her absolute favourite duellist. Unlike most prosecuting fencers, he delivers no florid speeches before the fight, nor does he parade around the court with a blue rose in his teeth after a victory. There is a cold beauty, a raw truthful-ness, to his style that is painful for me to witness as he slowly, methodically, and cruelly takes apart the convicted guard captain.

My fencing-master likes to remind his students, halfway through the interminable line drills when exhaustion has set our points to drooping and our legs to shake, that there is little difference between the profes-sional and the amateur at the beginning of a bout. Any half-trained fool can hold a proper guard and parry their way through the first few seconds of a match – perhaps even an entire minute. Only once the clock hand has begun to tick its way around its own circular court does the true duellist emerge, and the amateur realizes his folly. Our Lord of the Battering Blow knows precisely who is the duellist and who is the fool. But every time he tries to withdraw, to accept the new sentence that will see him past his best years before the sun ever touches his face again, the prosecuting solicitor shakes his head at Bézan Rechambeau, and Our Lord of Midnight once again wounds the defendant to add a year to his misery.

'Twenty-three!' The audience crows. 'Twenty-four!'

I hate this.

I hate the senseless callousness of it all.

Our Lord of the Battering Blow screams, a sound of such soul-breaking frustration and sorrow that I can't keep from clamping my hands over my ears. Having lost all hope, he throws his weapon at Bézan Rechambeau and runs at him, hoping to either overwhelm his opponent and snap his neck or, failing that, end his misery by taking a rapier thrust to the heart. There's a moment – just a brief flicker of pity in Our Lord of Midnight's eyes – that makes me think perhaps he will grant the guardsman the mercy of a quick death, but then he neatly steps aside. His point whips out to slice at the back of the defendant's ankle and a thin spray of blood paints the white marble floor. The big man falls to his knees, weeping.

It's over, I tell myself. It has to be over now.

But a twitch of movement catches my gaze. The prosecuting solicitor, standing outside the duelling circle, briefly holds up one finger and then three. Our Lord of Midnight hesitates, but the prosecutor repeats the gesture. Thirteen times more Bézan Rechambeau delivers nicks to the defendant's broad back. The audience – my good and true fellow citizens of Rijou – chant along with each blow. 'Thirty-four! Thirty-five! Thirty-seven!'

The guardsman doesn't even wail anymore. Like a dog beaten one too many times, the spark of his spirit has left the wreckage of his body to endure the unendurable.

'A suitable result,' My aunt declares when it's done. Even in the coldness of her painted lips I can't help but detect a stirring of desire, awakened within her as it is among the rest of the crowded courtroom. They say more babies are conceived in Rijou after a single day of trials than after an entire year's worth of drunken festivals elsewhere.

Aline, though she loves watching the duels and idolizes Bézan Rechambeau, looks sadly at the scene within the duelling circle. 'It wasn't right that the prosecutor made him keep going.' The words carry more naive confusion than judgment, which is strange to me because Aline, though third youngest of my many siblings, is the wisest person I know.

I don't know what comfort to offer her. The only present Aline wanted more for her birthday than to see Our Lord of Midnight fight in the duels is the gift that awaits her in the pocket of my jacket. I shouldn't give it to her, not after the way this trial's unfolded, but I can't stop myself. What I've purchased for Aline is only good for today, and it cost me every coin I could save for the last half-year. When she turns to speak to me, I hand her the delicately a carved ebony card etched in pure silver. Whatever she was planning to say dies on her lips and her face lights up.

'A dolvetto?' she asks, reaching for it. Her hand trembles. 'But which one?'

'His, of course,' I nod to the duelling circle where Bézan Rechambeau awaits. The reason the dolvetto was so expensive is that Our Lord of Midnight is notorious for never wanting to meet with the public. When I went to the duelling chambers that employs him they warned me the cost would be high, and whatever greeting I got for my money would likely make me regret my choice of fencer. But the unexpected joy on Aline's face is like a rope thrown to me before a raging river can pull me beneath its surface. I grab on tight. 'Go on then,' I tell her. 'The dolvetto is good for one hour, and there's an empty duelling court where he'll teach you whatever you ask.'

Other boys and girls – along with a few adults – are also holding dolvetto cards in their hands, eager to meet whichever court duellist they've hired for private lessons today. Aline begins to climb over the railing, so eager to run along with the others and meet her hero that she doesn't even make for the gate first.

'Stay where you are,' aunt Valoise hisses, grabbing at the back of the black and silver dress Aline insisted on wearing today in tribute to Bézan's signature duelling vest. 'You will not embarrass your family today, not in my presence!'

The collar of Aline's dress chokes her, and she falls back from the railing, unable to catch her balance. I step behind her, catching her just in time to keep her from tumbling to the marble floor. She smiles a thank you and, with graceful steps that strike me as more mocking of our aunt's arrogance than acquiescence to her expectations, proceeds to the gate and beyond to the duelling circle to present her ebony-and-silver token to her hero.

I turn to my aunt, my own smile gone now. 'Why must you be cruel to your own niece? It's Aline's birthday. Let her have one day free of your conniving and carping.'

Aunt Valoise doesn't sneer when she responds. Sneering makes faces unattractive, she always says. 'A niece would have to be the daughter of my brother, would she not?' Valoise asks pleasantly.

That poison drips from her lips to my ear, the words paralyzing me with a power they should not possess. There's been gossip in our household lately that when Aline was conceived, my father was off leading an armed assault against a growing band of brigands on our eastern border. If that were true, Aline would be the product of adultery and considered a blight on our house's dignity. But surely my father would have expelled her from our family if that were true? And yet . . . he's never looked on her the same way he does his other sons and daughters.

'Insinuate such a foul lie again,' I say to my aunt, who is twice my age and ten times the intriguer I could ever hope to be, 'and I will make you regret it.'

My warning is pathetically vague. In Rijou, a proper threat is expected to be specific and elaborate – a lengthy extolling of the precise manner in which you will bring someone to ruin. Mine just makes Valoise chuckle and pat me on the cheek. 'Dearest Percevar,' she says, leaning forward to whisper in my ear. 'Allow your loving aunt – for *you* are, however regrettably, the true son of my brother – to offer you this small gift on your sixteenth birthday.'

'I want nothing fr—'

She cuts me off, pulling me in close. 'Grant me the privilege of teaching you the one lesson your father will never think to teach you, Percevar. It's not your cowardice that dooms fools such as yourself, but sentimentality. Take a good look at your "sister". Take what pleasure and pride you can in the joy you've brought her for her twelfth birthday. Perhaps you can carry that memory with you after she's gone.'

I start to shove Valoise away, but like a trained duellist, she's already anticipated my attack and glides back effortlessly.

'Oh, look,' she says, pointing. 'Aline is getting along famously with her gift.'

I hear a squeal from the crowded duelling circle and

spin on my heel. I can barely see through the backs of taller admirers chattering with the court duellists and each other. Ignoring Valoise's earlier admonishment, I clamber over the railing and shove people aside until at last, I see Aline looking up with a besotted gaze at Bézan Réchambeau. Our Lord of Midnight seems less irritated than I would've expected. When he speaks to her, he's polite, almost tender. But then he glances in my direction and gives a nod that is so small, so curt, that for reasons I cannot explain my heart goes cold. Then I realize why: he wasn't nodding at me. When I turn back towards the enclosed noble's section of the courtroom, Valoise is already looking away, seemingly engaged in an enthralling conversation with the same Margravina she was slandering minutes ago.

'Percé, Percé!' Aline calls to me, beckoning me to join her. 'You'll come to my fencing lesson with Bézan, won't you?'

There's a moment when my mouth opens to speak but no words come out. Aline, though the youngest in our family, has always been the cleverest. How else has she survived both the enmity of the sons and daughters of other families who wage undeclared wars with their own siblings as is tradition in Rijou? How else has she evaded Aunt Valoise's machinations against her these past years? And yet now, she's as guileless as a girl half her age being handed a new doll to play with.

The perfect gift, I think then. *Something she cherishes so much that for the first time her guard comes down and she allows herself to feel nothing but innocent happiness.*

All at once, it occurs to me that Aunt Valoise could

easily have convinced my mother to forbid me from giving Aline the dolvetto card. She's never been in favour of girls learning to fence, even though it's common practice in Rijou.

So why did Valoise not seek to interfere in Aline's joy as she so often does?

My eyes meet those of Bézan Réchambeau. His are a bright blue against the dark, almost ebony skin of his face. I can't see anything in them, nor in the flat line of his mouth. He gives away nothing, for such is the sublime skill of a great duellist. It's also his one mistake. Why would a man notorious for being rude to his admirers be deferential to a moon-struck girl of twelve now?

'The lesson is private,' he says in his accented Tristian without inflection.

Aline shrugs as if she's already expecting me not to want to witness her fencing lesson. She knows better than anyone in our family how much I despise swordplay and all its elegant cruelties.

'I'm coming,' I tell her, but my eyes are still locked on those of Our Lord of Midnight.

'I told you—'

I cut him off, holding out my hand. 'Then give back the dolvetto card.'

'Percevar!' Aline practically shouts.

Bézan Réchambeau's gaze flitters over my shoulder. Is it an idle glance as he contemplates whether the fee he'll earn from this exorbitantly expensive private lesson is worth the annoyance? Or is he seeking instruction from his true employer. 'As you wish,' he says at last, slipping the dolvetto card into the slender pocket of his duelling vest. 'Two will hardly require more effort than one.'

As he takes Aline's hand and leads her out of the crowded courtroom and into the hall where we'll walk down to an empty one for the lesson, there's a smile on his face as if all of this has proceeded exactly as planned.

2

THE LAUGHTER OF THE BLADE

E ven as we walk along the opulent, expansive hallways of the Court of Blades, with its tall alcoves on either side of the walls decorated with pedestals bearing white stone busts of famed magistrates and legendary duellists, it occurs to me that I could simply scream. There are plenty of people about, after all: plaintiffs and defendants awaiting trial, clerks and other functionaries buzzing about doing the business of the court, and even a few stragglers wandering about in search of entertainment. If my suspicions, however unfounded, about Bézan Réchambeau and his intentions are true, I should call out for help.

But call out what?

'Help! This man wasn't annoyed when we handed him a dolvetto card for a private lesson with my sister! He glanced over my shoulder and may have been signalling something to my aunt! Murderous calumny!

Despite how stupid it sounds and how much more

stupid I feel, I might do it anyway. It's not as if I'm above the appearance of hysterical cowardice, after all. But every time I so much as think about it, I see Aline, her expression so full of anticipation, so devoid of fear. She keeps smiling up at me and urging me on as if I were a trepidatious puppy she'd just brought home and was trying to draw me into her bedroom for treats and a cuddle.

It will be fine, I tell myself, my gaze always returning to Bézan. Surely Our Lord of Midnight wouldn't risk his reputation – to say nothing of his liberty – on some wanton assassination of a noble son and daughter of his adopted city.

'This chamber is ours,' he says, pushing open a gleaming, freshly polished oak door with elaborate bronze engraving on the front displaying a symbol made up of two swords crossed and beneath them two hands clasped. 'Your dolvetto gets you the finest practice room in the court.'

'Guild rules require that duellists be able to practice in quiet before a trial,' Aline tells me quietly as if it's a grand secret she's discovered.

Inside the chamber, I'm struck by how much it looks like a smaller version of one of the courtrooms. The floors are the same polished marble as those of the trial room we just left, with a tall, domed ceiling above and mahogany panelling all around us. The crimson circle inset into the floor is the exact same dimensions as that of the courtroom, which doesn't leave room for spectator's boxes in this more compact space. Instead, there are racks of weapons along the walls, including practice rapiers of varying blade lengths to suit the different heights of their wielders. There are other types of weapons as well, representing the variety of requirements a magistrate might set for a duel. Daggers, dirks, and stilettos; small, circular buckler shields and massive rectangular kite shields. Spears and halberds of all sorts. There are enough tools of violence here to equip the platoon my father hoped I would join on next week's border raid.

'Well, little girl?' Bézan asks as he gestures to the weapon racks. 'You've an hour of my time. What would you like to learn?'

She giggles as if he's made a joke. 'The rapier, of course.' She walks over to one of the racks and draws the shortest blade she can find. It's still far too long for her. 'The rapier is the truest duelling weapon.'

Bézan shakes his head at her. 'You're too small for such a sword. Too weak to hold it properly. You'll only embarrass yourself and waste my time. Besides, only amateurs glorify weapons.'

He's right, and I'd feel far better if she were to pick up a spear, which can be held in both hands and would keep the two of them farther apart. But for some reason, his tone aggravates me unexpectedly. 'Don't talk to my sister that way. If she wants to learn a few rapier tricks, what harm does it do you to teach her?'

A slight curl in Bézan's upper lip betrays his otherwise expressionless features. His fingers draw the dolvetto from his black and silver duelling vest's pocket. 'You think this trinket lets you order me about, boy?'

'Please,' Aline says, coming between us. 'I'll be happy to learn anything Our Lord of Midnight wishes to teach me.' Suddenly, as if inspiration has struck her, she adds, 'It needn't even be fencing. You could teach me the sublime essence of duelling!'

The sublime essence of duelling. It sounds like something she must've picked up in one of those ponderous old swordplay manuals she keeps reading in our father's study when he's off leading his troops into battle.

Yet, Bézan's surprised grin seems almost genuine. 'Ah, you mean the lesson that can only be learned once? The secret that no duelling expert, not even the legendary Bottio Erras, ever put down on paper?'

I have no idea what either of them is talking about, but Aline nods excitedly. 'Yes, please!'

The famously taciturn Bézan Réchambeau's attitude changes, shifting all at once from bored and belligerent to dramatically enthusiastic. He begins walking the crimson line of the circle, arms outstretched wide like one of the heralds who proclaims the duellists' qualities and achievements before a trial begins. His voice is rich and deep, nothing like the growling whispers he'd reluctantly uttered until now. 'Duelling is an art with no rules,' he tells us, taking his first step like a dancer walking onto the stage. 'In this, it is utterly unlike fencing . . .' – he pauses to make a dismissive, almost effete gesture with his left hand as if waving away a butterfly – '. . . which is far too full of rules.'

'But surely there are *some* rules to duelling,' Aline says, her voice full of theatrical incredulity. She thinks she's playing along with a grand and entertaining joke Bézan is making.

With his free hand, Our Lord of Midnight reaches out to Aline, who accepts his invitation. He takes her much smaller hand in his and twirls her round and round like the two of them are performing a *virtuadoré* for me. 'No, little one. No rules, only a single precept. A single *truth*. This is the sole law that governs all duellists. It is the lesson you can only learn once.'

'What is it?' Aline asks, her question filled with hopeful anticipation even as she staggers to a dizzied stop in the centre of the duelling circle. 'What is the lesson?'

Bézan resumes his perambulation around the duelling circle with effortless precision. 'Oh, it is different for each duellist. In fact, it's not so much a lesson as a dark and terrible discovery.'

'A what?' I ask before Aline can do so. My voice quavers. I don't know why, and yet, somehow, somewhere deep inside my belly, I *do* know why.

Our Lord of Midnight nods absently, taking another step. Even with his front heel placed right in front of the toe of his back foot, he still seems perfectly in balance. 'A discovery,' he repeats. 'A . . . feeling. It is distinct to each of us and comes in reaction to that moment in time just before our first duel begins and we realize that nothing we believed about ourselves was true. That we were petty minstrels, drunkenly repeating to ourselves the story of our natures that was first made up by our families when they pretended to love us. The lesson lies in the questions we finally ask ourselves at the precise instant when the answers are too late to do us any good.'

Aline, standing there at the centre of the circle, slowly pivoting on the soles of her feet to keep facing Bézan, looks confused for the first time. 'I don't think I understand. What does that mean?'

But Our Lord of Midnight isn't talking to her anymore. He's stopped moving, too, and now he's looking right at me. In his cold, merciless gaze, all the fears and trepidations I convinced myself were imaginary are suddenly made as real and hard as stone.

'Why would a duellist of my calibre agree to give a fencing lesson to a silly little girl?' he asks, still watching me. 'Why would the Lady Valoise – a very compelling woman, I must confess – have allowed the child she considers an embarrassment to further humiliate her family with pretensions of learning to duel?'

He stops talking, but it's only a pause; I can feel it. It's the last question that's about to cut deepest of all into what's left of my soul even before that ebony-hued rapier of his flies from his sheath, the point resting just beneath my sister's chin, kissing the tender flesh underneath.

'What's the difference between a professional duellist and a hired assassin?' Bézan asks me.

'Percé?' Aline asks, her voice barely a whisper as she doesn't dare move.

It's strange. I've known her since the day she was born, and only now does it occur to me that I've never heard my sister sound frightened before.

'You'll be arrested,' I say, my mouth suddenly so dry the words come out in a frog's croak. 'You'll be executed for murder.'

His blade unmoving as if the Gods themselves were holding it perfectly in place, Our Lord of Midnight shakes his head. 'An accident,' he tells me, as if delivering the opening lines of his defence. 'The idiot brother was distracting me in the middle of the lesson, and the foolish, over-eager girl tried to lunge at me, so desperate was she to earn my approval by scoring a point on me. Alas, she dove right into the point of my rapier. Barely an inch and a half, my Lord Magistrate, that was all the steel dug into her young neck, yet, tragically, it was enough. More than enough.'

Before I can even try to speak, he holds up a finger with his other hand. 'Her brother . . . oh, that reckless, unhinged boy. When he saw his sister lying on the floor, the blood pouring out from her neck, he ran at me. I tried to keep him back; that's why there are so many shallow wounds on him, Your Eminence. But he kept coming, and then – oh, how cruel are the Gods! – he stumbled and the fool managed to impale himself on his own sword!' Bézan's hand rises up, cupping one side of his mouth as if he's telling me a secret. 'The audience won't be able to help themselves from chortling at that one.'

I swallow, and I would swear I can already taste bitter, coppery blood. I keep expecting some kind of anger to overtake me – a righteous fury that will overcome my innate fear of Bézan's sword, his monstrous skill, and the fact that he can kill my sister with nothing more than the twitch of his hand.

But I don't feel any of those things.

Instead, I feel . . .

I feel . . .

It's like I'm weary, but not tired. There's no stiffness or weakness in my legs as I walk to the weapons rack behind me. There's no shaking in my arm as I remove a rapier with a blade the right length for my height. When I turned to face Our Lord of Midnight, the most feared duellist in a city that boasts the deadliest fencers in the country, my shoulders are relaxed as I raise my weapon into the first and simplest guard I was ever taught, preparing myself to die.

I force the corners of my mouth upwards into a smile as my eyes meet Aline's. She's a clever girl. When the fight begins, she'll race for the door and out into the hall. She'll shout for help and find the constables, or if not them, at least someone to witness Bézan's crime. There's nothing to stop him from killing her first and me next, of course. He's more than fast enough to complete his grizzly work before either of us can flee. That's why I make him hear the coldness of my voice, and witness the utter lack of expression on my face. The emptiness before him is a curiosity, almost mesmerizing. I am nothing now but the absence of the boy I was, and the man I might otherwise have become had I not met Our Lord of Midnight.

'Bézan Réchambeau,' I say quietly, that vaunted name commanding no emotion from me whatsoever anymore. 'Are you ready for your lesson?'

THE LESSON YOU ONLY LEARN ONCE

With impossible slowness, the tip of Bézan Réchambeau's rapier glides along a perfect, invisible line in the air, leaving behind only the faintest graze on Aline's neck: a pencil-thin red cut so shallow that not a single drop of blood drips from it. I doubt the wound will even leave a scar. The gleaming black point of his blade moves, now aiming for my chest as Bézan takes the first step towards me, drawn towards me as if the inconceivable arrogance of my challenge were a magnet tugging at his blade.

I wait for him, unmoving, almost disinterested until the very instant his sword is out of reach of my sister. When I lunge, it's with every ounce of strength and speed my body can produce. From the sole of my back foot, up my calf and along my thigh, through the muscles of my torso and into my opposite shoulder and arm – all of it driving the point of my blade towards Bézan's heart so swiftly I can hardly believe it's me holding the weapon.

Close . . . so close!

His slip to the right is like the darting of a tree snake, but there's a tear in the right sleeve of his white fencing shirt that wasn't there before. Orlo Abradi, Our Lord of the Battering Blow, never came so close to cutting Bézan as I just did.

It's the closest I'll ever come and we both know it.

Aline's small body running from the circle is a blur of black and silver silk as the tip of Bézan's rapier whips out at my face. It feels like the gentle brush of a summer breeze.

I retreat, my hand going reflexively to my cheek, the fingertips coming back with a trace of blood. It's only then that I notice the slight sting on my right shoulder and left thigh, and realize he'd cut me twice more even as I'd stumbled back.

How can any human being be so fast?

No – that's the wrong question. I'm thinking like a fencer, but that's all done with now. I'll never fence again. This is a duel, my first and last. I understand now what that means. Bézan's magnificent trio of cuts against me was a mistake on his part. His reactions are still tuned to the exigencies of the duella condamno when the challenge was to score multiple wounds without killing his opponent. Had he stabbed me through the heart with a single thrust, he could've gotten to Aline and killed her before she reached the door.

I give him a dismissive salute – an insult meant to draw his attention back to me. 'You're extraordinary, my lord,' I tell him without a trace of mockery in my voice.

'It's rare to meet someone who is all the things people say of him and nothing more.'

I can see in the fractional tension in Bezan's friendly smile that my subtle insinuation has cut him deeper than my blade ever will.

Seems I've learned one or two things from you after all, Aunt Valoise.

'Come on then, boy,' he says, dropping the point of his blade until it touches the floor. 'One last roll of the dice before the end.'

Even a mediocre student of fencing comes to develop a few tricks: moves and attacks at which they naturally perform better than most of their classmates. Despite my many flaws, I've always been good at the high feint on the inside line to a true attack on the lower outside line. There's a part of me even now that whispers in my ear that if I just strike fast enough, make sure my eyes go to the false target of his chest first and then snap the blade back down to just above his knee, I can cripple Bézan Réchambeau with the gambit. From there, I'll have all the time in the world to flee – or perhaps even kill him.

No. I can't fight to my strengths. They're nothing compared to those of a professional duellist. Instead, I must fight to his weaknesses.

Bézan's life is defined by rules and procedures. His feet know the measure of a duelling circle so well he could walk it blind and never step an inch outside its confines. So I begin by running away from the circle and towards the corner of the chamber farthest from the door. When I turn back to face him, he looks at me like I'm an idiot.

'What's the matter?' I taunt him. 'Afraid if you leave

the safety of your precious magic circle that all your so-called talents will abandon you?'

Bézan shrugs and walks towards me, the tip of his rapier dragging along the floor to show just how little he thinks of my attempt to discomfit him. Yet, as I watch his steps, I note that they become fractionally shorter as he gets farther from the circle as if his body doesn't want him getting trapped in a corner. He's accustomed to being in the centre of the room.

How long has it been since we began? Ten seconds? Five? How long will it take Aline to find someone who'll listen to her?

I launch a few flourishes at Bézan – wide, extravagant slashes so obvious that my fencing master would've slapped me for such sloppy blade work. But Bézan knows these are nothing but feints, so he doesn't even bother to parry them. Instead, he waits for the one true attack that never comes because I know it won't succeed.

'She was right about you,' he says to me then, even as he brings his rapier up into line with my chest and I know the end is near.

I wonder if he means my aunt, but I don't bother asking. I came to this corner for the second rack of weapons here. Despite everything that's happening and how it will surely end, I can't help but smile as I violate the first prohibition my fencing master ever taught us: I throw my sword at my opponent.

In addition to being hideously bad form for a gentle-man, it has almost no chance of working. Even an amateur could dodge such a clumsy maneuver. A fencer of Bézan's calibre can knock a thrown blade right out of the air.

But what about a half-dozen weapons?

Even before I'd finished throwing my rapier, I'd begun reaching out with my other hand to grab at the hilts of weapons in the rack. I come back first with a fighting dirk, which I hurl at him end over end. I don't bother to see if it hits since it assuredly won't. Instead, I grab the next thing I can find: a round buckler shield that I spin in the air at his face. The second it leaves my hand I run around behind the rack of weapons, my back to the wall, and throw even more bits and pieces at him.

'Clever,' he says, dodging almost effortlessly even as he gets closer and closer. 'You know this will never work, though, don't you? Hurl as many daggers and shields at me as you want. You'll never hit me. Too bad you don't have a crossbow.'

'Only amateurs glorify weapons,' I remind him.

Before he can respond, I press my back against the wall, bring my right foot up against one of the rack's steel braces, and push with all my strength. The rack topples forward, and Bézan's eyes widen in surprise for just a moment before the whole apparatus comes crashing down between us. Had he been a few inches closer, or a fraction of a second slower, he might've been caught underneath.

'Too bad,' he says.

'I win,' I tell him.

His smile is curious now. 'What makes you say that?'

I don't bother answering. He knows as well as I do that I've given my sister the time she needed to flee. By now

she'll have found a constable and told him of Bézan
Réchambeau's crime. He'll still kill me, but his lies about
this being an accident won't hold water with anyone. I
have mastered the lesson that can only be learned once,
discovering who I am beneath all my fears and hesita-
tions. I have traded my life for that of the sister I love no
matter whether we share a father or not.

I am at peace, maybe for the first time in my life.

'Happy birthday,' I say quietly as I await Bézan's thrust.

My words echo eerily in the duelling chamber . . . only,
that's not an echo. Too late I hear Aline's voice and see her
standing there by the door. It's closed, yet I didn't hear it
closing which means she never left.

'Saint Zhagev-who-sings-for-tears, Aline, you fool,
run! You've got to ru—'

Bézan's blackened blade drifts down towards the
polished marble floor, gently, like a leaf on the breeze,
almost disappointed. 'The hour's not up, you miss,' he
says. 'Was the lesson satisfactory?'

Aline's not looking at him when she replies. She's
looking at me. 'Yes, my Lord of Midnight. Most satisfactory, indeed.'

Without so much as a nod of acknowledgment, the
man who only seconds before, I was absolutely sure was
about to kill me, turns and strides out of the duelling
chamber. Even his footsteps sound disinterested in what
has taken place here.

I start to step out from behind the fallen weapons rack
only to catch my toe on the edge, swearing at the sudden
pain in my foot as I stumble. The only thing that keeps me
upright is the wall I've fallen onto.

'I'm sorry, Percé,' Aline says to me.

I can't feel the anger yet. I'm still too lost in that moment between fragile life and certain death. But I know there's a rage that going to rise up in me the likes of which I've never before experienced, and never would've imagined could be directed at my little sister.

'You set all this up,' I growl, rubbing at the ache on my toe as I lean against the back wall. I'm suddenly so tired I don't think I can keep myself from collapsing to the floor much longer. 'You tricked me into buying you the dolvetto for your birthday, then you worked out an arrangement with Bézan Réchambeau to make me believe he'd been hired by Aunt Valoise to assassinate you.'

'Yes.' The calm in Aline's voice distresses me. It's far too much like Bézan's.

'Why? Why would you do that to the only brother you have who loves you, Aline? Who would—'

'Because you're not my brother, Percevar. You're my half-brother.' Her head tilts to the side like a cat studying a butterfly. 'You know that, don't you? I am the offspring of our mother's adultery.'

'You can't know that.'

She smiles like I'm the child. She points to the too-long, somewhat crooked nose on her face, and the cleft in her chin that neither my father nor mother possess. 'Of course I can. Anyone who takes on look at me can see what you refuse to. And one day soon, someone, whether Aunt Valoise or one of our siblings, will come for me to ensure my existence doesn't taint your father's noble bloodline. That's just how things work in Rijou.'

'I wouldn't let them.'

Aline smiles then, but there are tears sliding down her cheeks. 'I know that.' All in a rush, she runs to me and throws her arms around my waist as she buries her face in my chest. 'But devotion isn't enough, not even yours. You've convinced everyone that you're some sort of coward who can't fight. How can you protect me from Aunt Valoise and those she'll use to hurt me if you don't even believe in yourself? They'd only come after you first to get you out of the way. This was . . . this was the only way I could force you to discover who you truly are, who I've always known you to be.'

The lesson you only learn once, I thought.

Despite my best intentions, my arms wrap around Aline's shoulders, pulling her closer to me, and despite the fact that I'd expected to be furious with her, I notice that I, too, am crying.

'Happy birthday, Percevar,' she says.

THE END

DANCE OF THE CHAMBERLAIN

A TALE OF THE GREATCOATS

SEBASTIEN de CASTELL

THE DANCE BEGINS . . .

When seemingly supernatural events intrude upon the King's Law, one man is entrusted with uncovering the truth and seeing justice done. But can even Estevar Borros explain the chamberlain dancing in a palace ballroom two weeks after his death?

1

THE DANGLING CORPSE

The chamberlain's corpse danced from a rope looped around a beautiful chandelier in a ballroom surrounded by opulence, stinking of death.

Danced.

At this moment, the movements in question appeared to be a *virtuadoré* – an especially intricate noble courtship dance that involved a great deal of heel turns and swaying arms.

'How is this even possible?' demanded the Viscount of Cajoulac, pacing along the pristinely polished oak boards of his specially sprung floor which made dancing upon it less of a hardship to his guests' knees.

Not the one hanging from the crystalline chandelier, of course.

'I mean it,' the slender, elaborately-attired Viscount insisted, pairing his outrage with a stomp from his emerald green silk with ivory lace shoe against the floor.

'How can a dead body be dancing – literally dancing without cease even as we stand here watching?'

Estevar Borros, the King's Crucible, chose not to answer, merely placed his hands over his belly, and allowed his fingers to drum a rhythm against the thick dark crimson leather of his greatcoat. In times past he would instead twist the beaded braids of the neatly trimmed and carefully oiled black beard that came down to the collar of his coat, but given the nature of the conundrum before him, drumming his fingers seemed a more fertile investigative methodology.

'Well?' the Viscount asked him.

There were three other people in the room – not counting the small herd of kneeling grey-robed clerics wearing black funerary cowls that bobbed up and down as they chanted disharmonious prayers to any number of Gods real or imagined. Estevar knew the Viscount's confidants would only speak over him if he attempted to offer an opinion before they had their turn.

'It is witchcraft, of course,' concluded the mountainous Sir Galleato, dressed in plate armour despite the unpleasant heat emanating from the ornately carved marble fireplace at the end of the hall as well as the lack of there being anyone with which to do battle. Except, perhaps, Estevar, who he periodically glared at from beneath his steel war helm. 'Black, bloody witchcraft.'

Blood isn't black, Estevar thought, as anyone who bothered to stick around long enough after killing a person to see what death looked like would know. But men like Sir Galleato did not remain to witness the results of their actions. They were too busy bragging about them to their fellow knights.

Leave it alone, Estevar told himself. Murders aren't solved by getting into brawls with armoured thugs.

'Could it be a trick?' asked Damina Melisende Jovien. 'Some kind of . . . pulleys or springs hidden inside the metal shaft of the chandelier descending from the ceiling?'

Melisende was an older woman, grey hair thinning somewhat beneath the gold circlet crowning her angular face. The bright claret, almost pink gown she wore tried too hard to accentuate her bosom, suggesting she was struggling to hold the Viscount's continued interest. Age was crueller to mistresses than to wives, Estevar had observed more than once.

'Do not waste our time with the nonsense of whores,' said Venerati Magni Lazare, pausing in his own loudly chanted prayers to rise up and kick one of his lesser clerics who'd apparently fallen asleep in his duties. The shaven-headed figure looked up and offered a surreptitious rude gesture to the Venerati's back.

Fourteen days is a long time to put on such vocal displays of piety, even for professionals.

'This is the work of the Gods themselves!' Venerati Lazare declared, pressing the back of one hand against the palm of the other and holding them up towards the dangling corpse in a symbol of religious prayer. 'Only by their hand is such a punishment possible!'

Estevar waited for the Viscount of Cajoulac to reprimand the priest for the insult to Damina Jovien. When the reprimand failed to come, he contemplated doing so himself.

Picking a fight with the local collection plate despot won't get you any answers, either, he reminded himself.

'Well?' demanded Viscount Cajoulac, ending at last his winding journey around the ballroom to plant himself in front of Estevar. 'Which is it?'

Estevar understood the question but didn't appreciate the Viscount's tone any more than the man's gaudy green and gold silk coat or his overly-perfumed blonde wig. 'What is that you ask, my Lord?' he asked.

The Viscount stomped an emerald shoe against the floor once again. 'Which is it, man? Witchcraft, some kind of mechanical contraption we can't see, or the will of the Gods? By what mysticism or trickery is my former chamberlain dancing from a rope attached to my chandelier?'

'Ah, that,' Estevar said, then went back to tapping his fingers against his belly. 'I've no idea. A mystery hidden in dark shadows that even the bright light of your indignity cannot illuminate.'

The Viscount's eyes narrowed, and it seemed he wasn't so much a fool that he couldn't tell when he was being mocked, however subtly.

'There, you see?' asked Venerati Magni Lazare, his silver and black robes – expensive ones, Estevar noted, swishing almost musically as he strode across the floor towards them. 'I told you allowing one of the boy King's filthy tatter-cloaks inside the Palace of Cajoulac was a fool's choice.' He slammed a fist into his palm with such righteous force as might put even Sir Galleato to shame. 'This is the judgment of the Gods!'

No engagement, Estevar warned himself. No distractions from the—

'Which Gods?' Estevar heard himself ask.

Damn it.

Venerati Magni stopped mid-stride. 'What?'

'Which Gods?' Estevar repeated. 'When I was a boy, newly arrived to this country, there were six. They went by different names depending on which Duchy you were in, but by and large one's prayers went to either Love, War, Death, Coin, Craft and . . . I forget, who was the sixth one again?'

'What is your point, Trattari?' the priest asked, using the derogatory term often employed to disparage the King's Travelling Magistrates.

'And then the Gods were all murdered, weren't they?' Estevar went on, ignoring both the question and the insult. 'All of a sudden we had only one God, but then, he turned out to be the God of Fear, which wasn't good for anyone, least of all the poor starving hordes driven to praise his ascension as the deity in question tore apart Castle Aramor and proclaimed himself ruler of all humanity.' Estevar turned at last and tilted his head as he examined the cleric. 'I believe I saw you there, did I not, Your Worship? I remember because your personal flock was so very large – in number, I mean, not in girth – as they appeared to be starving at the time.' Estevar locked eyes with Lazare.

Sir Galleato rose from the stool where he'd been seated, his armour clanging as he approached, pleased to have finally found a potential enemy to pummel. 'What would you know of starving, tatter-cloak? How on earth does a man as fat as you ever survive a duel?' A gauntleted hand gestured to the symbol of a cauldron inlaid into the left breast of Estevar's long leather greatcoat. 'Is that why they call you the "King's Pot"? On account of your belly?'

Estevar tut-tutted the Knight. 'You know, it's rather out of fashion to belittle another's physical appearance.'

Sir Galleato's grin made a cross from the slit of his steel helm. 'Not in these parts, it isn't.'

'I assure you it's so. I could introduce you to a string of gentlemen of your disposition from here to Aramor whose noses are most unfashionably shaped ever since they chose to comment on my girth. A curiously consistent outcome that I would be open to exploring further should you wish to assist me in my study of the phenomenon.'

'Please,' interjected Damina Jovien, 'arguing amongst ourselves will not solve the murder of this poor man.'

'Nor clear the stench from my ballroom,' muttered the Viscount of Cajoulac. He glanced up at the dead chamberlain. 'Poor Prissard. He did so love to dance. I always did have trouble getting him out of here at the end of a grand ball.'

The corpse seemed to agree, arms weaving in the air to unheard music as it pirouetted around its tether, the tails of the blue embroidered chamberlain's coat flapping elegantly while the crystals of the chandelier tinkled together as if toasting each other's health. Despite being two weeks dead and somewhat the paler for it, the chamberlain appeared much like any living forty-year-old man – save for the vacant stare and the mouth hanging agape in an expression of fright and horror.

'Your man, Prissard, he had no wife, no family?' Estevar asked.

The Viscount shook his head and sighed. 'His life was his work, this palace.'

'And no one has been able to remove the body?'

The Viscount's expression turned sour. 'Sixteen of my servants have made the attempt since the night we discovered the body. The moment any of them came too close, they were stricken insensate by some sort of spiritual assault that left them incoherent for hours. I assumed it was a case of cowardice causing them to faint, but then I tried myself and was so overwhelmed with panic I nearly knocked myself unconscious. Even attempting to cut the rope using a serrated blade attached to an eight-foot pole failed to offer any protection. I hoped perhaps someone made of sterner stuff would overcome the curse, which is why I summoned Sir Galleato.'

The Knight's expression lost its smugness. Apparently, Galleato's virtue had proved no more potent than that of the palace servants.

'It is as I have advised you,' Venerati Magni Lazare began, seizing the reins of the debate once again. 'By the will of the Gods does this damned soul writhe above us. Punished for these lustful, sacrilegious, and execrable dances you allow to take place in your home.' He then gestured to the nearly two dozen kneeling clerics braying their endless prayers from inside their cowls. 'And only by securing the Gods' forgiveness will the curse be ended.'

'Yes, damn you, but how?' asked the Viscount. 'I've already made another sizeable donation to your church. What more do the Gods demand of me?'

Here it comes, Estevar thought.

Lazare stepped forward and took the Viscount's hands in his as a father might a child's for whom he must now report that the family cat has, alas, gone to a better place. 'I fear, my Lord, that only through purification and consecration can this palace once again find favour with the Gods.'

'You mean . . .'

Lazare nodded sadly. 'You must withdraw from this place for a time, my Lord, perhaps to your winter home? I will bring to this doomed place a hundred priests, each of whom will live here day and night, praying and performing sacrifices in your name until the Gods relent.' Before the Viscount could object, Lazare added, 'Fear you not, my Lord. Already I have begun plans to conscript fifty new Church Knights who will lend soul and steel to the defence of this palace, and keep out any who might seek to invade it.'

Including the Viscount of Cajoulac himself, Estevar thought.

It was an old game, though one attempted less often these days now that the churches had fallen into disrepute. One had to admire the Venerati Magni's brazenness, if not anything else about the man.

The Viscount looked up at the dancing corpse hanging from his chandelier, who had now switched to a less formal country jig. Lazare, seeing his opening, gripped the Viscount's hands so tightly he winced. 'I have the papers prepared, my Lord. Merely sign them and we can begin the healing of both your palace and your good name.'

That last part was the cleverest. Should word spread of this curse upon the House of Cajoulac, the Viscount's reputation would surely be ruined beyond repair. And spread it would, rather quickly, with the two dozen priests Lazare had brought with him to shout it from the rooftops of every church in the Duchy.

Cajoulac looked as if he might well be ready to give in, ignoring the pleading gaze of Damina Jovien, whose counsel, it seemed, the Viscount had abandoned of late along with her bed.

Right then, Estevar thought. *Enough flouncing around. Time to get to work.*

Before the Venerati Lazare could put quill and ink into the Viscount's trembling hands, Estevar said, 'You'll need a Magistrate to witness the contract. Otherwise, it will be open to dispute.' Estevar made a show of examining his fingernails. 'I have it on good authority that the new King of Tristia takes the non-hereditary transfer of capitals of Duchies, Demesnes, Condates and Marches quite seriously. It would be regrettable if he should decide that the Viscount's newfound . . . piety constituted abdication and used his royal prerogative to name someone new to the position.'

Venerati Lazare didn't like the sound of that one bit.

'I would be happy to witness the contract myself,' Estevar went on, 'being as I am, in fact, one of the King's own Magistrates.'

'Fine, fine,' Lazare said. 'Then let us do so and resolve this mat—'

'. . . once the appropriate legal formalities are concluded,' Estevar said.

They were all looking at him now: Venerati Lazare, Viscount Cajoulac, Sir Galleato, Damina Jovien. Even a few of the two dozen priests had ceased their Gods-awful chanting to see how Estevar would answer the obvious next question.

'Legal formalities?' the Viscount asked.

Now, Estevar thought. *Now is the time to set us all straight. You've all had your say, my worthies, so I will have mine.*

'A trial, my Lord,' he replied. Before any of them could object, he raised a hand, and let them see in his countenance that despite how they might have viewed him up until this moment, a Greatcoat was not to be trifled with. 'Let us clear up a few facts, shall we?' he said, and began his own perambulation around the centre of the ballroom, his steps slow but sure, each one beating out the rhythm of his words, making sure they would not forget what next he told them.

'I have listened to your speculations, Sir Galleato, Damina Jovien, and Venerati Lazare, now let me provide you with a few incontestable facts. First, regardless of the means by which the chamberlain's corpse now dances above our heads, the man himself was murdered. Second, as a member of the King's Order of Travelling Magistrates, I require no invitation to investigate a crime of such magnitude.' Estevar rested his hands on the lapels of his coat. 'Third, make no mistake my Lords and Lady, I will identify the perpetrator and hold him to account, and any who seek to gainsay my verdict, whether a soldier, a priest, or one of the Gods themselves, will meet me in the duelling circle and learn for themselves why the King entrusted me with this coat.'

'By all the Saints!' Lazare roared, turning his ire on the Viscount. 'Who is this arrogant windbag you allow to make a mockery of your court?'

Estevar answered for himself.

'My name is Estevar Valejan Duerisi Borros, sometimes called the King's Crucible, both because it is easier to remember and because it is I that his Majesty entrusts to investigate matters of the supernatural. And it is I who will discern both the means and the perpetrator of this foul deed. Now, quickly, someone bring me a violin.'

'A violin?' Sir Galleato asked. 'What on earth for?'

Estevar turned to resume his study of the corpse whose continued dancing defied the laws of nature but would not, Estevar swore, defy those of humanity. 'So that I may interrogate the witness, of course.'

2

THE VIOLIN

The instrument was passable, but not of the finest quality. When first he placed it to his shoulder and let the bow caress its strings, the sound was halfway between a dying man's groan and the screech of a cat in heat. Estevar's father had always been disappointed in his son's failure to take his music lessons seriously.

'How can this possibly work?' Viscount Cajoulac asked, holding his palms against his ears as he stood alongside his three advisors and the two dozen chanting priests. None of them appeared impressed by Estevar's musical skills.

'It is a simple matter of reason, my Lord,' he replied, drawing the bow against the strings a second time. The result was better. Somewhat.

The ballroom's long oval shape and its supporting columns created wonderfully complex reverberations. The chamber was a masterpiece of architecture – deserving of a far better performance than it was getting today. Estevar took a moment to improve the angle of his elbow, straightened his back, and tried to imagine his own violin teacher breathing down his neck as she was wont to do during their lessons.

'You see,' he went on, pacing around the dangling corpse as he tried a third stroke that proved even unluckier than the first two. Undaunted, he continued. 'A Magistrate – even one of my particular speciality – trades not in skepticism any more than superstition. I do not consider the metaphysical implications of the evidence before me, only its veracity.'

The fourth note he tried to pull from the violin's strings – now that one he had to admit was truly hideous.

'Oh, give me that,' Damina Jovien said, coming to take the instrument from him. 'You'll no doubt raise more of the dead the way you're going.'

Estevar ceded the violin to her and gave a small bow to her as she began tuning the pegs with considerably more deftness than his own clumsy attempts.

'She seemed quick to involve herself,' Sir Galleato said, drawing an absurdly wide longsword from its sheath. With two hands on the hilt, he aimed its point at the dancing corpse before lowering it in the direction of Damina Jovien's neck. 'Everyone here knows Prissard, the chamberlain, wanted her out of the palace. He was spreading rumours about her to the whole court!'

'What sort of rumours might those have been?' Estevar inquired casually.

Viscount Cajoulac coughed. 'I don't see that we need t—'

But the Knight was too filled with glee to heed his

politically weak Lord's counsel. 'Prissard was telling anyone who was listening that she was diseased . . .' the point of his sword aimed at the Damina lowered even further. 'Down there!'

Estevar watched for her reaction, admired her composure, and resolved to see the stain of gossip removed from her reputation when this matter was dealt with – unless, of course, she turned out to be the murderer.

'And what of you, Sir Galleato?' Damina Jovien asked, aiming the violin bow in his direction as if she might cross blades with him. 'Was it only I who witnessed you bullying Prissard all those nights? Drunkenly demanding favours for your lesser Knights? Threatening to beat him in front of his elderly and emotionally fragile mother unless he acceded to your demands?'

Behind his steel helm, Galleato put on the disdainful smirk that no doubt served him well on the battlefield when he needed to mask his fears. His eyes followed the line of his sword below the silver belt of the Damina's pink gown. 'I've heard witches get all sorts of diseases down there, don't they?' His head swivelled to seek out support from Venerati Lazare.

'I have encountered many practitioners of witchcraft,' Estevar observed. 'Both authentic and those purveyors of fakery. Most of the genuine ones are decent men and women whose arts provide healing and aid in birthing or the growing of crops.' He winked at one of the priests who looked particularly aghast at this calm description of witchcraft. 'Along with a few naughtier spells, of course.'

Venerati Lazare clenched his fists and looked very much as if he wanted to meet this upstart Greatcoat in a

duelling circle. Estevar guessed the lithe and broad-shoul-
dered cleric would prove a more dangerous opponent
than Sir Galleato with his bulky armour and preposter-
ously heavy longsword.

'What a witch's magic cannot do,' Estevar went on,
pointing to the still-dancing corpse. 'Is keep a dead body
animated for fourteen days without sign of decay or the
presence of insects. Look you, my Lords and Lady, for
there should be flecks of the chamberlain's flesh dripping
from his bones right now – especially with all those
gyrations.'

There was a groan from the priests, and one of them
vomited. This, in turn, prompted two more to empty the
contents of their stomachs on the Viscount's lovely
polished dance floor.

'So then it's not magic?' Damina Jovien asked, testing
her tuning of the violin with a stroke of the bow across its
strings. The chord was lovely, almost sublime in the
magnificent acoustics of the ballroom.

Estevar smiled at her but shook his head. 'No, my
Lady, nor does the answer lie in your insightful conjecture
regarding a mechanical source to the conundrum
dangling above us.' He removed one of the short leather
straps with iron spikes from his coat. 'Despite my size, I'm
a more than adequate climber, and the vines growing up
the exterior of the palace provide an excellent means of
ascent. There is no apparatus hidden on the vaulted roof.'
He put the climbing strap away. 'Though it was a wise
instinct, my Lady. Trickery often veils itself in mysticism,
as we all know.' He allowed himself a second wink, this
time at Venerati Lazare's expense.

'Why, you arrogant wret—'

'Ah, yes,' Estevar said as if the priest had helpfully reminded him of something he'd forgotten. 'The matter of the Gods. Well, it may please you to hear that your insistence that this is a matter of divine intervention is, in fact, correct.'

Every movement in the room, every sound – including the still-chanting monks – came to an abrupt stop.

'What?' Viscount Cajoulac asked.

'Indeed,' Estevar confirmed. 'You see, as we learned two years ago when the Gods were ingeniously murdered so that a new deity could take their place – and further demonstrated when the Greatcoats tried and executed that same pernicious God of Fear for his crimes – divinity in our troubled country is a matter of . . . faith.'

'What do you mean?' Damina Jovien asked, the violin bow now hanging limply from her side. 'You're saying the Gods aren't eternal?'

'Alas, no, my Lady.' He thumped a foot against the floor. 'The ores beneath the ground in many parts of Tristia – the ones our ancestors were first brought here as slaves to mine – they possess an unusual property. They can transform the focused will of a people into manifested power bearing the attributes of those desires.'

'You mean . . . that which is prayed for comes to life?'

Estevar nodded, though somewhat sadly. He'd been quite religious as a boy. 'The first prayer came before the first God, and we all get the Gods we deserve. Alas, it also means curses can, at times, carry a great weight here in Tristia.'

Viscount Cajoulac stared up at the corpse of his chamberlain. 'But what does that have to do with Prissard dancing up a storm fourteen days after someone killed him?'

Estevar motioned for Damina Jovien to prepare to play. 'That is easily explained. You see, after the murder of the old Gods and the subsequent execution of the new one, the force that gives them life was dispersed across Tristia. Now, the Gods have begun to return, of course. We've had unconfirmed reports of Love, Death, and a new God of Valour in the past two years, but they are still . . . young, we might say. Their power isn't fully concentrated.' He looked up at the body of the chamberlain, which was now performing a sombre pas dei chatelles. 'We've seen many such phenomena of late. Some call them curses, but my studies suggest the mystical forces summoned, act as a kind of . . . counter-balance – meeting one form of emotional energy with its spiritual opposite.'

Damina Jovien was the first of them to understand. 'But if Prissard's corpse is dancing merrily, then wouldn't that mean . . .'

Estevar gently took the hand that was holding onto the bow and raised it to meet the strings. 'It means our poor chamberlain met a death so foul that the energies from which the Gods themselves are made rages against it, and only by finding the killer may we put his soul, and this very palace, to rest. Now play, my Lady, and pray you, play exactly as I instruct, for you and I tamper with the forces of life and death now.'

3

THE DANCE

'Given the particular manifestation of the energies at work among us,' Estevar began, clasping his hands over his belly as Damina Jovien waited for his instructions on what to play, 'we may surmise that he was murdered the night of the Viscount's last ball.'

'We knew that much,' Sir Galleato said with a snort. 'His body was found here after it ended. What else could it have been connected to other than the ball?'

'A marvellous insight,' Estevar said. 'Nothing at all, other than perhaps every single other event of note to take place in the Demesne of Cajoulac. You are truly a wonder, Sir Galleato.'

The Knight wasn't pleased, but a look from the Viscount kept him quiet.

'Now, my Lord,' Estevar said to Cajoulac, bidding him to come closer. 'What was the first dance of the night?'

'There were twelve dances that night. The first was a . . . a pivousette, I believe.'

'It was,' Damina Jovien confirmed. 'You and I danced it together, my Lord.'

'If you wouldn't mind?' Estevar said to her, motioning for her to play.

The lines buried beneath her thick maschiera paints revealed themselves as the Damina's expression grew troubled. 'Do I risk my soul with these actions? I would not wish to dabble in the dark arts.'

'Fear not for your soul,' Venerati Lazare said, his words dripping with disdain. 'Its fate was set long ago.'

'Madam?' Estevar asked.

She looked up at him, still holding the violin on her shoulder and the bow to its strings. 'Yes, Magistrate?'

'It is not my place to interpose myself in your affairs, but as a man of the Law, it is only right that I should remind you that in this Duchy, three insults of the same nature to an individual's honour affords the right of duel. Should you desire to avail yourself of this traditional privilege, I would be most content to offer my services as your champion, or, if you prefer to remonstrate the bleating prat in the gaudy silk robes yourself, I would be honoured to serve as your second.'

Lazare's face betrayed little, nor did he bluster at Estevar's threat, yet the man's stance widened, one foot a few inches in front of the other.

So, spent some time training as a warrior, eh? Estevar observed. It seems your ambitions have always leaned to the temporal rather than merely spiritual, Venerati.

As for Damina Jovien, she did not smile at Estevar's offer, nor did she take offence at his cavalier words. The Damina, he now suspected, had her own plans for dealing with Venerati Lazare when the time came, and Estevar wished her every success in that endeavour.

'Well, then,' he said, 'with my assurance that you commit no offence against nature, my Lady, might you favour us with a pivousette?'

Damina Jovien began to play, and even in these gloomy and sinister circumstances, her performance was lovely. The melody was crisp, the rhythm moving. The corpse above them stopped its dancing and hung limp.

'How is that—' Viscount Cajoulac began, but Estevar shushed him.

'Continue, please, my Lady,' he instructed. He turned to the others assembled on the other side of the ballroom. 'Who here knows how to dance the pivousette?'

Sir Galleato raised his hand, as did a few among the priests – to the angry glare of Venerati Lazare.

'Excellent,' said Estevar, and he took up a position on the dance floor, gesturing for Sir Galleato to join him. 'Would you prefer to lead or follow? I'm an excellent dance partner and can perform either role.'

'I'll not dance with a man!' Galleato growled.

'Yes, of course,' Estevar said, nodding. 'Wouldn't want to get infected down there. Very well, I suppose it's easier for me to think if I'm leading, anyway.' He directed his attention to the priests. 'Might there be a lady among you who knows her dance steps?'

'Women are barred from the priesthood in the Duchy of Domaris!' Lazare declared. 'Unlike those libertine Duchies who surround us with their wickedness!'

'Yes, well, here's your problem, my good Venerati, you see, when you create a job as cushy as that of cleric, collecting tithes from folk with barely enough to feed themselves and living off rich food and drink while they suffer, some folks – libertines, I suppose – decide they'd prefer that lifestyle to the one you'd consign them to. Of course, I imagine true religious fervour is hard to find these days, what with the people of Tristia still reeling from the destruction caused by the God of Fear who those, like yourself, Venerati, however innocently helped to create. So your recruitment process is, I suspect, somewhat laxer these past two years. And since a further innovation among your particular ministries is enforced celibacy, well, you see, it becomes rather difficult to know who's who, and somewhat easier to illicitly join your church.'

Before the Venerati could dispute the impertinent speculation, Estevar turned to the Viscount. 'Have I your permission, my Lord?'

One had to give this to the besieged nobleman: he was cannier than he let on. 'If it removes a curse from my palace without me giving it away to the bloody priests, do as you must.'

'Outstanding.' Estevar returned to the priests, who were all glancing at each other with renewed curiosity. 'Now, madam, I will not reveal you without your permission, nor allow the Venerati here to perform any unannounced . . . inspections. However, if you would be so kind as to assist me presently then the Viscount will provide you with a lifelong position in his household with a substantial pension.'

'You insult my churches,' Venerati Lazare said, taking a position between Estevar and the priests. 'You insult the Gods themselves. I'll not allow you to demean my prie—'

'Oh, do shut up,' said one of the robed clerics, rising up from her kneeling colleagues. She strode past Lazare and came to stand before Estevar. 'I was mostly trying to hide out from a charge of cattle theft, anyway. Wasn't planning on staying long. I'll expect a pardon for that.'

'No Viscount's pardon protects the soul of an apostate,' Lazare said, though not loudly, which made the implied threat against her all the more sinister.

She pulled down the cowl to reveal a smooth face that couldn't have seen more than eighteen years. Her head had been shorn like those of the other priests, and the loose robes along with her square jaw had likely assisted her in passing as a man. 'Ain't my soul but my belly what complains when it's empty,' she called back to Lazare. 'Now you,' she said to Estevar. 'How about we talk pardons and salaries?'

He found himself grinning at the brazen woman standing before him, fists on her hips. 'That depends on how well you dance, my dear. Your name, if you please?'

'You can call me Coral,' she replied, making it plain that her true name was none of his business.

Estevar held out a hand for her. 'Shall we begin?'

She gave him a passable curtsey before accepting his hand. With Damina Jovien ably playing her violin, the dance began. As Estevar led his new partner in the first steps of the pivousette, the dead chamberlain began to scream.

4

THE INTERROGATION

'Fear!' the corpse howled. 'What price pays the one who replaced life and love with terror and dread in this body, who amidst joy abundant and unbounded desecrated that which was through spirit united and sanctified?'

'What in the name of Saint Zhagev-who-sings-for-tears is he on about?' asked Coral as Estevar led her in a spin on the polished oak dance floor. 'Sounds like he's talkin' about a religious rite, not some poncey ballroom gala.'

Ah, exactly! Estevar thought as he spun the shaven-headed young woman through the middle measures of the pivousette. *All those bodies, those spirits, dancing joyously together. Not so different from a shared act of ritual prayer.*

'Murder!' the corpse howled again.

'Who killed you?' the Viscount called out. 'Tell us Prissard, and I swear the villain will hang for it!'

But the body of the dead chamberlain slackened against the rope.

'Quickly,' Estevar ordered. 'The next dance, what was it?'

'A . . . shimonze, I think,' the Viscount mumbled.

'No, that was third. It was a troup-delouse,' said Sir Galleato, then, as he saw the others staring at him, grumbled, 'It's no sin for a Knight to enjoy dancing.'

Venerati Lazare might've contested that assertion from the expression he wore, but Estevar had more urgent lines of inquiry to pursue. 'Damina Jovien, if you will?'

The Damina gave barely a breath's pause before she switched her playing to a faster rhythm, the melody punctuated by flicks of the bow against the violin's strings. The troup-delouse was a more rustic and less familiar dance to Estevar, who preferred the classics himself. Fortunately, the false priest dancing with him recognized the tune immediately and guided him well enough.

'You pick up the moves pretty well for such a big fella,' she observed after the opening measures.

'I am blessed with an excellent partne—'

'Corruption!' the corpse screamed in outrage. 'With smiles and grins were dark bargains offered. Those who refused purchased their own slaughter.'

'What's this about corruption?' Sir Galleato asked.

But the corpse had stopped moving again.

'The shimonze, yes?' Estevar asked the Knight. 'That was the third?'

After a nod from Sir Galleato, the Damina Jovien shifted to a new song, this one blessedly slower. Coral clearly wasn't familiar with it, but the young woman was clever; she merely stood on his feet and made him carry her through the dance.

'Speak, dread spirit!' Venerati Lazare said. 'As the most blessed seneschal of the Gods in this mortal domain, I command you to speak the truth and only truth in this place ere I allow you to your eternal rest!'

Coral rolled her eyes. Estevar restrained his smile. While it was easy to dismiss the way some of the clergy so casually manipulated their flocks, the price paid by the faithful was far too high.

'Violence!' the corpse replied with a baying that shook the rafters of the ballroom's vaulted ceiling. 'As dancers revelled and others sought secret places in which to delight in one another's flesh, one who wished only for such pleasures met with suffering and death!'

Again the body seemed to collapse, hanging limply from the rope, and again Estevar asked for the next dance from that evening.

'A bella soiré,' Damina Jovien replied, but when she changed her tune to the slower, more intimate rhythm, the body remained silent.

'What's wrong?' Coral asked as Estevar stopped dancing. 'Did she get the wrong one?'

'I think not,' he replied. 'I pray you, my Lady,' he said to Damina Jovien, 'play for us the next song.'

It was a simple country jig, but even before Estevar and Coral took their first steps, he sensed it wasn't working.

'The next, if you please,' he said.

She did as he asked, but there were no more howls, no more revelations; the corpse simply began following its own dance once again. The same occurred with the next, and the one after, and the one after that.

'That's it then?' Sir Galleato asked. 'Someone threatened Prissard, that was during the pivousette, then during the troup-delouse there was some kind of corrupt goings-on, and after that, during the shimonze, they killed him?'

'But that tells us nothing!' the Viscount of Cajoulac cried out. 'We know no more now than we did at the start!'

That was enough to launch Venerati Lazare into a victory speech on the futility of mortals treading upon matters best left to the Gods and their chosen representatives on earth. Sir Galleato, apparently a recent convert to more reasoned lines of inquiry, tried to argue otherwise. Estevar let them have their spat. Experience had taught him it was best to let blowhards huff and puff a while.

'You think there's more to it?' Coral asked, watching his eyes.

'I do. Tell me, my dear, have you much experience with murder?'

She arched an eyebrow at him. 'Are you accusin' me of something, Greatcoat?'

'No, no, I merely wonder . . . during your time as a priest, did you ever assist in the performance of funeral rites for a murderer?'

She shook her head. 'Murderers and traitors don't get ceremonial burial in the Duchy of Domaris. It's the opposite – the priests perform what's called a contra-benediction upon their bodies. Their flesh is scored with a short spike, once for each of the hells to which they're being consigned. The priest spits inside each wound as an act of desecration.'

An act of desecration! That's the answer!

Estevar was so overjoyed he nearly took the liberty of kissing the young false priest on the forehead, but reminded himself the customary traditions of his home Duchy of Baern were not shared in other parts of the country.

'What's that look in your eye?' Coral asked. 'You're grinning like a cat what's got the mouse he's been chasing all day cornered.'

'Indeed,' Estevar agreed. 'That is precisely what this smile means.'

The arguments and accusations flying between Venerati Lazare, Sir Galleato, and Damina Jovien had now expanded to include the Viscount of Cajoulac himself, who they suggested might've murdered his own chamberlain to hide his recent financial losses and that the expensive balls were his way of luring wealthy nobles to his home where he could ply them with drink and attempt to manoeuvre them into backing his next ventures. Meanwhile, the nearly two dozen priests had resumed kneeling in prayer, though it seemed now what they begged of the Gods was to liberate them from this place.

Such liberation would not be forthcoming.

Estevar stepped away from Coral, took a deep breath, and in his most commanding – and voluminous – tone bellowed, 'Seal the doors!'

The room fell to silence.

'Why?' asked the Viscount. 'Why? If one of us is the murderer, the others will surely stop them from fleeing.'

'Seal the doors,' Estevar repeated, then walked to the side of the ballroom and dragged a chair back to the centre. It wasn't a proper Magistrate's throne, but it would do. He unbuttoned his coat, took his seat, and announced, 'The trial is about to begin.'

5

THE TRIAL

The four suspects, Damina Melisende Jovien, Sir Galleato, Venerati Magni Lazare, and the Viscount of Cajoulac himself, stood before Estevar, who sat placidly on what had turned out to be a surprisingly comfortable chair. Behind them, the two dozen chanting priests – well, minus Coral, of course – watched the proceedings with confusion.

It must have galled them all, Estevar thought, *to bear witness to a mere Greatcoat commanding the obedience of four such powerful figures.*

Well, we all have our vexations to bear, do we not, my friends?

'How do you propose to render a judgment,' asked Sir Galleato. 'Given we've all seen everything you saw, heard what you heard, and none of us could name the killer or anything about them with what little we know?'

'Ah, well, as to that, we stopped our experiment a tad too early, I'm afraid.'

'What?' Damina Jovien asked. 'But you said—'

'My Lady, if I might beg you to take up the violin once again?'

Coral, standing next to Estevar's chair, groaned. 'This again? No offence, Your Eminence, but you were starting to get a little sweaty by the third dance.'

'Fear not, my dear. The paired dances are of no further use to us.'

Of all of them, only Damina Jovien picked up on the distinction. 'You mean the group promenades? There were only two. I started playing the first one earlier, but nothing happened.'

'The second, it takes place at the end of the night, I take it?' Estevar asked.

She nodded. 'At midnight, always at midnight, like the old folk traditions to close off a festival celebration.'

'Blasphemy,' Venerati Lazare muttered.

'Indeed,' Estevar agreed, and gestured for Damina Jovien to take up the violin she'd left balanced on the elegant green-upholstered chair next to her. 'If you wouldn't mind, my dear?'

She did, then frowned a moment. 'I've never played a promenada florajis before. I'll have to improvise it from memory. It may not be very good.'

Estevar leaned back in his chair to glance up at the smoothly swaying corpse of Prissard, the chamberlain who in life had loved to dance, and through dance was his life stolen from him and his soul desecrated.

'I don't think the witness will be too picky.'

Damina Jovien set the bow to the strings. 'Now?' she asked.

'Not quite yet,' Estevar answered.

He summoned Coral to him, whispered quietly to her. When she'd heard his instructions, she stared at him with wide eyes a moment. He gave her a reassuring nod, and she went to the back wall of the ballroom and took down three of the House of Cajoulac's ceremonial swords.

'Sir Galleato is already armed with his magnificent longsword,' Estevar explained as Coral handed out the weapons to the other three. 'It is only fair the rest of you should be similarly equipped.'

'So it's you!' Venerati Lazare said, grabbing the broadsword from Coral's hand and raising it up into a more than passable guard as he spun on Sir Galleato. Once again, the priest's martial training revealed itself. 'You're the murderer! That's why the Greatcoat wants us armed, so the three of us can stop you from escaping!'

'I'm no—'

Lacking a Magistrate's bell, Estevar rammed the hilt of his own rapier against the arm of his chair. The thud echoed throughout the voluminous ballroom.

'My friends, I ask that you remember that as of right now, this is a courtroom. My courtroom. I will hear the final testimony, and then I will render the verdict. Until then, you will comport yourselves civilly.' He leaned forward in his chair, his rapier still in hand. 'Unless one of you wishes to challenge me, first?'

No doubt at least two of them would normally consider such a proposition, but for now, they all knew the real danger wasn't Estevar, but the others in the ballroom with them. Yet still, every single one of them failed to see the real threat in their midst.

'No takers?' he asked, but was met with silence save for the creaking of the rope attached to the slain chamberlain's neck as he danced alone to music only he could hear.

Patience, my friend, he told the dead man. What peace justice and truth may bring, on my oath as a Greatcoat I will soon deliver to you.

'Now,' he said, loud enough to command the room. 'I believe I am on solid ground in my assumption that the promenada florajis – the "promenade of winter flowers" is a group dance so common that anyone who's either born to this Duchy or has lived here any length of time would know it?'

'The steps are simple and known to all,' Damina Jovien confirmed. 'Children learn it from a young age, and it's performed at weddings and festivals. It requires at least four dancers, however.'

'Wait a second,' Sir Galleato interrupted, gesturing to himself and the other three next to him. 'Don't tell me you expect the four of us to dance together?' He held up his longsword. 'While carrying weapons?'

Estevar waved away the objection. 'Fear not, Sir Knight, it is not my practice to force suspects to risk skewering each other with the pointy end of a sword, though I admit, it has its merits as an expedited form of jurisprudence.'

'If not us,' the Viscount said, 'then who is supposed to—'

He, like the rest of them, understood then what Estevar was proposing. The four of them turned to the two dozen confused monks staring up at them from their kneeling positions.

'Even priests had to have been children once, didn't they?' Estevar asked rhetorically. 'And I'm told they're often found at weddings.' He caught their attention with a wave of his hand. 'Rise, brothers. The Gods request the pleasure of your company in this final dance of the evening.'

6

THE FINAL TESTIMONY

A few of the priests tried to object, hoping no doubt to cite the blasphemy of being required to perform a heathen dance, but Venerati Magni Lazare's icy glare silenced them, and the curt nod of his head sent them to the centre of the ballroom, where Coral directed them to their positions.

'They're as ready as they're ever going to be,' she told Estevar.

He motioned for her to come to his chair. When she did, he whispered to her something he'd forgotten to earlier. 'My dear, I have a pair of daggers in my coat. Would you like to borrow th—'

She opened the sleeve of her robes, and there he saw strapped to her forearm a stiletto blade. 'I've been sleeping in a tiny stone cell surrounded by men for nearly six months,' she said quietly. 'You think I wasn't ready in case one of them decided I was a little too pretty for a priest?'

'I begin to suspect, my dear, that there is no situation for which you are not always prepared.'

She patted his cheek. 'Smart boy. Now pull off a miracle and solve this, would you? I'm eager to move into the lovely quarters you're going to make the Viscount of Cajoulac give to me as part of my new job. Assuming he's not the killer, of course.'

She was clever enough not to expect an answer and stepped back to stand outside the ring of priests where she could clap the rhythm and shout the steps to them. Without requiring further cue, Damina Jovien played the first few notes of a light yet stately tune.

'Step to your neighbour, turn to your right,' Coral called out. 'Bow to the soil, hail to the stars. Spin-on your heel, stop on the left, blow a kiss to the wind, shed a tear for the rain.'

The priests – most of them, anyway – did a passable job of following the moves. Damina Jovien's playing was tentative at first, but she soon found her confidence, which made it easier for the dancers to follow the tune.

Come on, Estevar pleaded silently with the corpse hanging above him, which had ceased its own swaying but hadn't yet uttered a sound. *I've given you the dance you were waiting for, as much a spell as any cast by a mage. Awaken for me once more, Prissard, and let's make an end of this together.*

'Nothing's happening,' Sir Galleato said.

His soldier's instincts were no doubt warning him what would happen if the guilty party wasn't to be revealed through these means, for Estevar saw him sidle a few inches away from the others to give him the distance to bring up his sword should they turn on him.

'Shall we stop?' Damina Jovien asked.

'No, damn you all!' Estevar said, rising from his throne. 'Keep dancing!' he shouted to those among the priests who were starting to ignore Coral's calls. Turning to look up at the dead chamberlain he raised his fist and yelled, 'I am Estevar Valejan Duerisi Borros, a duly sworn Magistrate of the King of Tristia. This trial is under my jurisdiction, and by the laws reconsecrated at Aramor by Aline, daughter of Paelis that did by her voice bind even the Gods, so do I command the witness to answer my question. Prissard, Chamberlain of Palace Cajoulac, tell this court what was done to you after your death!'

The room was still for a moment, even with the thumping of the priests dancing, even with Coral's clapping to the melody of Damina Jovien's violin. But then, Estevar saw the corpse's lips part, and the unnatural howl that erupted from its mouth shattered the windows throughout the ballroom and sent knife-like shards of glass raining down upon the oak floor.

'DESECRATION!' it screamed.

7

THE VERDICT

The priests stopped moving. Coral stopped clapping and Damina Jovien set down the violin and bow, taking up the sword Coral had provided her earlier in its place.

'Desecration,' the corpse repeated, though now the shrieks had become a piteous wail. 'Monstrous sacrilege performed as planned, and he of virtue thus thrice-damned.'

'What does that—'

But the Viscount's question was cut off when the chamberlain's body fell silent for the last time. His body stripped of unnatural life, turned like any piece of dead meat would, until suddenly the rope that had kept it there fourteen days gave way, and the corpse fell to the floor with a crashing thud.

'By all the Gods,' Venerati Lazare swore, and this time, he sounded genuinely prayerful.

Estevar Borros felt the weight of Prissard's murder

upon him and marvelled that what had been done to him afterwards was somehow an even viler act.

'I will now rule on this case,' he said, then had to repeat himself because he'd barely mumbled the words on his first attempt. He steeled himself, fingers doing up the buttons of his coat once more before he turned to face Viscount Cajoulac, Sir Galleato, Venerati Lazare, and Damina Jovien, all of whom held the swords provided them in their hands, all of whom wondered upon which of them those blades would soon turn.

'A chamberlain is a powerful man,' Estevar began, watching the beams of light through the shattered windows dance against the blade of his rapier. 'More powerful, some would say, even than the Lord he serves, for the chamberlain manages the purse, directs the guards, guides the day-to-day life of not only the palace but all those whose livelihoods depend on its commerce.' He locked eyes with the Viscount. 'And he has one other power, too. Perhaps the greatest of them all. The power to sway his Lord to one course of action or another.'

'What are you accusing me of?' Cajoulac demanded. 'You think I—'

'I think nothing, my Lord. I know. I know you didn't kill your chamberlain, because he refused to do as he was asked by those who wished him to trick you into abdicating your own palace.'

'The palace?' Damina Jovien asked. 'You mean . . .'

She, the Viscount, and Sir Galleato turned on Lazare at once. 'You bastard,' the Knight swore. 'You wanted Palace Cajoulac. You came here with that decree all ready to go!'

The Venerati Magni's outrage gave way to genuine fear. He knew no words of his would deter the three of them.

'The conspirator is not Lazare,' said Estevar. He held up a hand before Damina Jovien or Galleato could object. 'Neither is it either of you, Sir Knight, my Lady.'

'Then who?' the Viscount asked, practically squealing the question. 'Unless . . .' he pointed to the body of chamberlain on the floor. 'Somehow Prissard . . .'

'No,' Estevar said. 'Prissard was, as the curse that kept him dancing before you these past two weeks told us, free of any guilt. Venerati Lazare did indeed long to possess the Palace Cajoulac. It isn't so rare a deed. Many nobles have been persuaded over the centuries to give away a castle here or there in favour of winning better treatment in the afterlife. The fact that Venerati Lazare was one of the three summoned to advise the Viscount after his chamberlain died indicates he is, indeed, concerned with such eternal matters. But the Venerati is not so vile a man, nor does he possess the means by himself to summon and channel the forces by which the supernatural is governed here in Tristia.'

Estevar began walking into the centre of the cowled and robed priests. 'But you did, didn't you, brothers? Most clerics have fled their faiths since the God of Fear made a mockery of blind devotion. Some remained because they refused to believe what had taken place at Aramor, others believed they could redeem religion by staying true to the Gods they once worshiped and who we now believe rise again. A few, though . . . well, it should've occurred to me much sooner that a few would have seen what was possible using ritual and faith and, instead of being horrified by it, see opportunity unfold.'

One of the priests made a lunge for him, but Estevar's blade was at the man's throat before he got within four feet of him. 'I think not, my friend.'

He continued his march along the circumference of their line. 'To achieve great ends requires great numbers, which you did not have. Yet, you craved the luxurious life that would have been yours had Venerati Lazare succeeded in convincing the Viscount to render unto your order this palace. The Venerati would've risen higher, and each of you, perhaps, given new titles and ranks. But being compassionate men, you first offered Prissard a choice: push the Viscount into turning over the palace and its lands to the Church, or face a fate worse than any death.'

Estevar's route had brought him back to the body on the floor.

'The chamberlain was, I fear, too honest a man, and his reaction must have instantly told you he would not only refuse you but reveal your foul intentions. So you slew him, and afterwards, as the revellers in this ballroom performed the promenada florajis, a ritual ancient and venerated in this Duchy, you performed your own rites upon Prissard's body.'

Estevar raised up his rapier and slashed down at the body on the floor, the tip slicing through the dead man's coat and shirt, revealing the marked flesh beneath that had been hidden because until now any who attempted to tamper with the body were struck down by the spiritual forces surrounding it.

'You all made these incisions into his flesh with cere-monial spikes. You spit inside the wounds and muttered curses against him. You brought him here in the dead of night when the dance was done and hung him here to haunt this room.'

Estevar turned to Lazare. 'And it was these men who came to you, did they not, Venerati, and persuaded you that the Gods themselves must have laid their punish-ment upon the Viscount for his refusal to see that they desired this place to be not a palace hosting blasphemous dances, but a cathedral consecrated to their glorification?'

'I . . . No,' Lazare said, but then hesitated. 'And yet . . .' he pointed to one of the robed priests. 'You came to me three days ago while I was in prayer.' His arm swung to another of the priests. 'And you begged me to allow the papers to be drawn up in case the Viscount should decide to . . .' The hand that wasn't pointing at the conspirators, the one holding the sword Coral had given him at Este-var's instruction, rose up high as Lazare shouted a war cry against his own flock.

The priests weren't caught unawares. Several had weapons secreted upon their persons and by mute agree-ment determined then and there that none but they would leave this room alive. But it is one thing to have a weapon and another to be expert in its use.

'By my authority as a Greatcoat do I find you guilty,' Estevar said, raising the blade of his rapier. 'The sentence, I regret to inform you, is death.'

They turned on him, surrounded as he was by their far superior numbers. But Estevar's distraction only served to make them turn their backs on Viscount

Cajoulac, Damina Jovien, Sir Galleato, Venerati Lazare, and Coral with her stilleto, each of whom was a far more skilled fighter.

Six of the priests went down before any of them had so much as attempted a thrust. The next six went down almost as quickly. A few of the others got in lucky blows. Estevar caught a dagger thrust aimed at his heart that left him gasping for breath but failed to pierce the bone plate sewn inside the lining. Damina Jovien was the eldest among them, but she took only a shallow cut to the arm she'd been using to defend herself. The Viscount himself suffered the worst injury: a deep stab to his leg that bled profusely.

'Stop your bleating,' Coral yelled at Cajoulac as the rest of them fought off the remaining priests and she wrapped a hastily torn strip from the Viscount's coat around the wound. 'It's not like I'm going to let my new employer die before he's even given me my first promotion.'

The end came swiftly after that, and soon the beautiful polished oak floor of the Palace of Cajoulac was a tapestry of grey and scarlet. The most dangerous part of the battle proved to be stopping Venerati Lazare from butchering every last one of them. Some of his ire, Estevar knew, was at himself, for surely it said something that all these traitors found themselves united in his church instead of another's.

'It is enough now,' Estevar said, holding the powerful man's arms behind his back. 'The living are done with these men. Let the dead have their turn.'

8

THE BURIAL

I t *was a nice service*, Estevar thought as they stood among the crowds of Cajoulac's people as Prissard was laid to rest. Venerati Lazare had – politely, for once – requested to deliver the sermon. The Viscount had, equally politely, refused, asking instead that his new probationary chamberlain do so.

Coral did a rather fine job of it, though her speech contained more curses than one expects to hear at a funeral.

'Prissard would've loved that,' the Viscount said to Estevar confidentially afterwards. 'He was always a trifle irreverent. One reason I kept him around, I suppose, even though he annoyed me at every opportunity – he annoyed Lazare even more, and kept me from making mad deals when he could.'

'He was not the only one who tried, however,' Damina Jovien observed wryly.

The Viscount took her hand, and a wink passed

between them that suggested the beginnings of reconciliation – or at least a conversation on the topic.

Estevar smiled, and laughed, though he didn't feel much like doing either. There was an exhaustion that took him at the end of a particularly difficult case, and the joys that followed came from sharing the tale of it with fellow Greatcoats back at Aramor. Men and women who understood how precarious a commodity justice was in Tristia.

So perhaps it was the will of some divine influence that had Coral walking beside him as he made his way to the stable where his mule awaited.

'There's one thing I don't understand,' she said, holding onto his arm as if they were young lovers strolling by the seaside. 'How did you know I wasn't involved with them? I mean, shouldn't you at least suspect I knew about the plot?'

Estevar started to put his hand over hers, then thought better of it and stuck it in the pocket of his greatcoat. 'The answer to both questions is the same, though I doubt it will make you happy.'

'Tell me.'

He stopped and turned to her. He decided they were good enough friends despite the short length of their acquaintance for him to give her a small kiss on the cheek. He was relieved when, instead of punching him, she blushed.

'Your beauty is, I fear, not quite so easy to hide as you believed, my dear, and men not quite so foolish as you would like to believe. The other priests figured out you were a woman. That's why they kept their plans from you yet never revealed your deception to Lazare. You were their backup plan. Should anyone discover their conspiracy before they could enact it, they would claim the plot was yours.'

Coral shook her head and uttered one more curse.

'A woman,' she said, mimicking Lazare's indignant zealotry. 'A whore, hidden among us, spreading deceit and devilish plots! To the fires with her!'

'One hopes his recent experiences will temper his religious fervour,' Estevar said, though without much conviction.

Coral glanced back at the church grounds and the crowds assembled there. 'Somehow I doubt it. Say . . .' she began, in the elongated vowels of a teenager about to ask a parent for a loan. 'Just in case this chamberlain business gets boring, how hard is it for a girl to sneak her way into the King's Travelling Magistrates?'

Estevar tilted his head in confusion. 'Does the news really not reach this part of Domaris at all?' he asked. 'The First Cantor of the Greatcoats is a young woman by the name of Chalmers.'

Coral stared at him wide-eyed. 'A woman?'

Estevar nodded. 'All of eighteen years old.'

She grabbed his arm. 'Wait a minute, you're telling me you – all of you Greatcoats – take orders from a woman my age?'

Estevar wasn't sure how to address that tone. 'I assure you, Chalmers is a very remarkable young woman whose valour and wise judgment is beyond question,' he insisted. 'Such qualities are hard enough to find in this troubled nation of ours, and in no greater supply in one gender than another. To be one of the King's Travelling Magistrates is to—'

'Yeah, yeah,' Coral said, turning to head back towards the church where the Viscount awaited his new chamberlain. 'Tell that Chalmers of yours to watch her back. After I fix this dump up a little, I might be coming for her job.'

Estevar watched her leave, then finally clasped his hands over his belly and resumed his walk towards the stables, muttering to himself all the while, 'Gods protect us all.'

THE END

GRAVE OF THORNS

A TALE OF THE GREATCOATS

SEBASTIEN de CASTELL

THE PRICE OF BETRAYAL

Murielle de Vierre was once the King's Thorn, a loyal member of the legendary swordfighting magistrates known as the Greatcoats. But a single poor choice turned her into a traitor, and set her on a path that led far from the ideals to which she'd once held. Now she wanders alone, disgraced and despised, searching for the road home.

1

THE PRIZE FIGHTER

My first mistake was in letting my opponent enter the duelling ring ahead of me. The minute the big man had ducked under one of the frayed ropes tied around six rusted iron posts that marked off the fifteen-foot hexagon inside which we'd be fighting, he took up a position on the western-most corner. In the village of Phan, prizefights began an hour before sunset when villagers returning from their labours could witness the show without having to waste expensive oil for lanterns.

The problem for me was that put the sun in the west and therefore right in my eyes when I faced the six-foot-six man-shaped boulder who now grinned from one misshapen ear to the other as he cracked knuckles that could probably smash through oak planks with ease.

The fight master, a slender, moustachioed wine merchant who wore what I assumed were his festival colours of green and gold, leaned uncomfortably close to me. 'You'll have to remove your coat, my lady,' he said, wiping the sweat and dust from his brow with a dirty rag.

Like a yawn spreading through the crowd of onlookers, the villagers likewise rubbed at faces and forearms in an endless battle with the dust that blew in from the Eastern Desert – the enemy next door that threatened daily to bury everyone and everything beneath its sands. Hard to imagine anyone choosing to live here, but then, dying here wasn't such a good idea either.

'The coat stays on,' I said, nodding to the big lout waiting to bash my skull in with fists bigger than any blacksmith's hammer. 'That padded leather jerkin he's wearing offers no less protection than my coat.'

That part was a lie, of course, but occasionally it works.

The fight master started tapping at the dark grey leather of my greatcoat as he listed off its various offences. 'Thin, flexible, and nearly unbreakable bone plates sewn into the lining,' he said, rapping his knuckles against my chest. His hands slid down to my waist. 'A hundred or so hidden pockets. Spiked caltrops to drop on the ground at your opponent's feet when nobody's looking? Powdered amberlight to blind him? Perhaps even a square of that legendary hard candy that gives you Greatcoats unnatural strength and vigour in battle?' His right hand drifted to the end of my sleeve. 'I imagine you still keep a few of those inch-long throwing blades secreted in your cuffs, don't you? Wasn't that why they used to call you the King's Thorn? On account of the way you could flick those tiny finger blades into an enemy's face or sword hand?'

'You seem to know an unhealthy amount about me,' I said.

The fight master smiled as he spread his arms wide as if to encompass the entirety of this sad little village by the desert. 'Oh, we have plenty of history with the King's Travelling Magistrates here in Phan, my lady.' He bent forward to whisper conspiratorially in my ear. 'Not a happy history, mind you.'

I pitched my reply loud enough for the crowd to hear me. 'I told you all before, I didn't come here looking for trouble.' I gestured to the small hill less than an eighth of a mile to the north overlooking the village. 'I came solely to visit the King's grave. Though why any monarch would choose to be buried in this backwater that lacks for anything worth visiting – even water – remains a mystery to me.'

My diplomatic skills firmly established, the villagers returned my courtesy by hurling clods of sand-filled turf at me, most of which landed on the fight master's gaudy waistcoat.

'Our guest seems to be having trouble removing her coat,' he announced with loud, boisterous good humour as he turned away from me and towards the crowd. 'Shall we show her our hospitality and assist her in—'

He stopped talking when he felt the sharpened point of an inch-long blade at the back of his neck.

'You were right about the finger knives,' I whispered.

The fight master waved off the half dozen especially eager members of the audience coming forward to separate me from my coat.

'Can't stop you from killing me, if that's your desire,'

he whispered back. 'But if you hope to visit your King's final resting place with your skin intact, then you'll provide the citizens of this "backwater" village, as you call it, with a few meagre minutes of entertainment. I doubt even a known traitor such as yourself would sully the efforts of the new First Cantor of the Greatcoats to rebuild your order's already tarnished reputation by slaughtering an entire village.' The fight master turned to face me, forcing me to either remove the blade from his throat or risk slicing it open. 'Now, my lady,' he said, 'are you going to remove that coat of yours and make this a fair fight or not?'

A fair fight.

The man standing opposite me in the roped-off hexagon who'd introduced himself as Brudal Rofslough – despite everyone else referring to him simply as 'Brutal' – was a dark-haired, wild-bearded monstrosity who stood a foot taller than me and weighed at least a hundred and fifty pounds more. His padded jerkin was sleeveless to accommodate shoulders so wide they would've ripped through the leather. Should either of those big hands of his catch hold of me, I'd quickly find myself at his mercy – of which I doubted he was in great supply.

But then, I hadn't travelled five hundred miles to this sweltering, barely habitable dust bowl searching for mercy.

I unbuttoned my coat and slid it off my shoulders, folding it carefully before setting it on the ground on the other side of one of the iron posts.

The fight master's easy smile returned. 'Will you

herald yourself, my lady? Or might I have the honour of doing so on your behalf?'

'You go ahead,' I said, shifting right and left a few inches, getting used to the loose soil underfoot and seeking out a spot where the setting sun wouldn't be in my eyes. Alas, no such relief awaited me, so I decided to use what time I had to examine how my opponent moved and whether he really was as eager to pummel my bones to powder as he appeared.

The fight master beamed at my reply as if I'd confirmed his heralding skills were so widely admired that even I, a snobbish foreigner from the south, had heard of his talents.

'My Lords and Ladies!' he began, pivoting on his heel to face the crowd.

'No Lord or Lady had likely passed through the non-existent gates of this turd of a village in decades,' I muttered.

Undaunted, he gesticulated grandly towards my opponent. 'Our favourite son you know already. Brudal is undefeated in the ring . . .' the fight master raised his open palm to his mouth and whispered loudly, ' . . . or in the bed, or so I've heard it said!'

That line earned him polite rumbles of laughter that suggested this wasn't the first time he'd leaned on it. What he said next, though, proved him a shrewder hawker than I'd anticipated.

'Quit talking shite,' Brudal said, glowering at the fight master then at me. 'She wants to visit her dead King's grave? I'll gladly arrange it.'

The fight master treated the interruption as the transition to the next act of his play. 'Ah, but could there be dangers lurking ahead for our paragon?' he asked the crowd, adding a bewildered and almost despairing tone to his words. 'Yet, surely no one is stronger or braver than Phan's own champion?'

Outraged denial erupted from the crowd.

'Oh,' the fight master went on with a dismissive wave of his hand, 'perhaps when forced to contend with fancy weapons requiring years of expensive training, someone born to honest labour might be at a disadvantage . . .'

The space he left was filled with boos from the adults and laughter from the children.

Let them jeer, I thought. *It's nothing I haven't heard a thousand times these past months.*

'But we fight honestly in these parts,' the fight master declared. 'Hand to hand, fist to fist, beneath the eyes of the Gods themselves!'

Roars of approval. Someone started passing out mugs of beer as men and women began thumping their feet on the dusty ground, the rhythm of war drums before the battle.

'So it's not with raw strength or a righteous heart that a warrior of Phan can be defeated.' The fight master jabbed an accusing finger to where my coat lay folded on the ground outside the ring. 'Nor fancy weapons or tricks.'

Now even the children were booing.

Saint Eloria-whose-screams-draw-blood, how badly do these people hate Greatcoats? I wondered, keeping an eye on Brudal, guessing at the length of his stride which foot his weight would be on when we met in the centre of the ring.

'No, my friends,' the fight master went on. 'A foe needs

different weapons to defeat a champion of Phan.' His mouth twisted into an ugly grimace. 'Corruption and guile. Cruel cunning and unbridled villainy, that's how honourable folks like us meet dark ends.'

The grumbles rising up from the audience threatened to become growls.

The fight master's performance was masterful. He wasn't merely introducing two fighters, but retelling the myths of this village. Phan wasn't some pitiful, impoverished collection of cottages stuck on the edge of a desert. This was a crestfallen army, encased in cracked armour, suffering one unjust defeat after another by the vile machinations of unscrupulous invaders. They saw themselves in Brudal: big and strong, too simple and honest to be anything but virtuous, bravely facing the vile, despicable...

'Murielle de Vierre!' the fight master said my name as if it belonged to the evil villainess of a thousand tavern tales. 'If there is one woman whose nefarious wickedness could slither inside our walls and wrest unjust victory from the time-honoured traditions of noble combat, it is surely she who so arrogantly calls herself The King's Thorn!'

I hadn't called myself that in a long time. Nonetheless, I stepped forward, assuming we were about to get to the actual punching part. Regrettably, the fight master was only getting started.

'Know you, my brethren,' he began – a roadside cleric unleashing the fire and brimstone of his sermon – 'that this...' he paused as a disgusted expression contorted his lips, '. . . *woman*, if such a name still fits if only because no other suits her, is no mere *Trattari*.'

The word meant 'tatter-cloak' and was the favoured epithet used against the Order of King's Travelling Magistrates. I'd always rather like it. *Trattari*. Sounds like a type of flower.

'No, brothers and sisters,' he went on. 'Even among their meddling, despicable company is Murielle de Vierre reviled.' He wagged a finger in the air as if to forestall denials no one was making. 'I speak not of the rumours – though there are many – that she earned her coat not by the skill of her arm or the righteousness of her verdicts, but by talents she displayed best on her back!'

The sight of mothers covering the ears of the children they'd brought to share in the entertainment of watching a five-foot-six woman getting her head bashed in by a brute three times her size was starting to annoy me.

'Get on with it,' I muttered.

Brudal, shuffling and snorting like a bull waiting to be released from its pen, seemed to agree with me.

The fight master either didn't hear me or didn't care.

'No, such unseemly rumours – however justified – are of no interest to the good folk of Phan,' he intoned judiciously. 'What troubles our souls is that even amongst the Greatcoats, the King's Thorn stands out.'

He turned and strode back towards me with such fervour the audience no doubt wondered if he'd decided to fight me himself. The fingers of his right hand reached out to touch my hair in a fashion that badly wanted for them to be broken. I couldn't take the bait, though.

'Not for these scarlet curls,' he said.

His fingertips brushed my cheeks.

'Nor the beauty that brought Viscounts and Margraves to their knees as they plead with her to marry them.'

Suddenly his hand came back and I thought he might actually slap me. Instead, he merely tilted it clockwise as if presenting me at a Ducal ball. His voice softened, became gentle, yet still was loud enough to be heard by all as he rendered the final indictment. 'When a would-be despot rose up and threatened to bring the barbarian hordes of Avares to invade our peaceful country when the same Greatcoats we'd rightly reviled over the years none-theless found the courage and decency to stand against him, to put their very lives on the line for those of our people, do you know what this woman, this Murielle de Vierre – said to be one of the King's favourites – did?'

He held the silence with a raised fist, and only when it seemed the crowd would faint from having forgotten to breathe so long, did the fight master answer his own ques-tion: 'She sided with the tyrant.'

He didn't need to call for the fight to begin after that, merely walked over to one of the ropes enclosing the hexagonal duelling ring and step beneath.

He was clever, this one: he'd ensured those last words would be the ones in everyone's minds as a man three times my size strode across the dirt and sand to break me into pieces before their eyes.

She sided with the tyrant.

2

THE FIGHT

Among the Greatcoats, for whom duelling in all its forms is as integral as knowledge of the King's Laws, three were generally acknowledged to be the toughest opponents: Kest Murrowson, Talia Venire, and Falcio val Mond.

Kest was known as the King's Blade because there was no one alive more skilled with a sword. I'm told he even became the actual *Saint* of Swords for a while. Kest never much liked me.

Talia, the King's Spear, had the virtue of complete lunacy and a craving for warfare so deep that should someone manage to one day kill her in battle, she'll surely rise from the grave the next morning to stab them through the belly out of sheer spite. Talia never much liked me, either.

Falcio val Mond didn't seem to mind my company. Named the King's Heart because he, more than any of us, embodied the idealism on which the Greatcoats were founded, Falcio was the canniest duellist I'd ever met. If an opponent were faster than him, he'd find a way to turn that speed to his own advantage. If the enemy were stronger, Falcio would trick him into smashing his fist into a stonewall or break the blade of his sword in a reckless swing. Falcio didn't need to be the fastest, the strongest, or the most skilled. He was simply the best.

As for me? Among the Greatcoats, I was known as 'the pretty one'.

Brudal's fist came for my jaw like a bolt of lightning hurled from an angry sky. Instinct and sanity begged me to leap out of the way, but the training Falcio had given me taught me to duck underneath the blow and slip to his right flank. I had an opening to drive my elbow into his ribs, but instead, I took two quick steps, pivoted on my heel, and waited for Brudal to turn before pairing a sultry smile with a sly wink.

'You're beautiful,' Falcio had told me once when we were sparring in the Greatcoats training hall. He was the only one back then willing to spend any time training me. 'Use it. Seduce the enemy.'

I painfully rose from the cold marble floor where he'd knocked me down for the third time, took up the same guard position that had failed me twice already, and spat. 'That's insulting. You think King Paelis named me to the Greatcoats because I'm pretty?'

Falcio sometimes blushed when he caught me staring at him. Not this time. His reply was as cold and quick as his sudden lunge for my open line. 'The sharp end of a rapier doesn't give a shit whether the King gave you a coat thanks to your keen intellect and noble spirit or because he secretly wants you in his bed.' As I parried, he turned my blade away, came in close, and punched me in the shoulder so badly I lost my grip on my own sword again. 'The bony end of a fist doesn't care, either.'

I knelt down, retrieved my weapon, and faced him once again. 'And what do you care about, Falcio?' I asked, blinking away tears.

He smiled. 'Better,' he said, and brought his rapier back into line. 'Now make me believe it.'

I'd screamed at him then, unleashed the frustration of nine months among men and women I admired more than any others in the world who looked down on me as a plaything brought among their number by a young King beloved for his compassion and decency yet notorious for his romantic appetites. I brought my blade up high for a reckless diagonal slash only to then hurl it at Falcio.

'That's a stupid—'

Even as he batted it away, I dove to the floor, rolled into a somersault that brought me up beneath his sword arm. Before he could react, I smashed my fist into the inside of his wrist. His rapier clattered to the floor.

Falcio was mostly known for his swordplay, but there was no part of combat for which he wasn't prepared. He quickly grabbed hold of my forearms – an inefficient lock meant to show me that I lacked the strength to escape.

'You had five disabling targets,' he informed me. 'Eyes, throat, nose, nerve clusters on the inner thigh, and, in case you've forgotten, the groin. You went for the disarm because it's a flashy manoeuvre and you wanted to prove you can win on skill and cunning alone.'

Since he seemed so disappointed with my point of

attack, I drove my knee up for a groin strike, but he was ready for it and raised his own to block me.

'Now you've taken the target I wanted you to go for simply because I put it last on the list and emphasized it. Control the fight, Murielle. Don't be controlled by it.'

'I can do anyth—'

He cut me off with a glare. You could almost smell the speech that was coming.

'I'm not interested in how tough you think you are any more than I care how weak others will mistake you for being. There's nothing to prove in the duelling circle. When we fight, it's not just our lives on the line but the verdicts we render. Other people – people without skills or training or even your looks – they're the ones whose rights depend on us winning. You want to be a Magistrate? A *Greatcoat*? Then you've got to win your damned fights. An opponent lusts after you because you're pretty? Distract them. Someone resents you because they mistake your looks for privilege? Let them seethe with hatred until it makes them sloppy. Win clean, win dirty, humiliate yourself or others, I don't care.' He squeezed my arms tighter, causing me to flinch. 'Just come back alive.'

He let go of me, and his eyes went to the places on my arms where his fingers had gripped me.

He's looking for bruises, I realized. *That's Falcio's weakness: despite all his pretence at dispassion, all his talk of equality, he's terrified of hurting women.*

How he knew what I was thinking, I couldn't tell. I guess there was a reason why King Paelis had named Falcio as his First Cantor of the Greatcoats.

'Good,' Falcio said. 'You've got the eye of a duellist. Let them guide you.'

I found that unexpectedly funny. 'So I should not only make use of my looks to seduce an opponent but also play on my apparent weakness? Is that the kind of Greatcoat you want me to be, Falcio?'

'You think there's something noble about being gifted with exceptional strength or speed? Kest refused to even pick up a sword before he was twelve. Within a year he was practically unbeatable. We're born as we are, Murielle, and a Magistrate fighting to uphold a verdict that will affect the lives of dozens or even thousands who can't afford shame or guilt. To a duellist, everything is a weapon or a weakness. If you want to survive this job, you'd better learn to make use of them all.'

Sound advice. Too bad he forgot to add, *'and never get so lost in nostalgic recollections that you give your opponent the time to bash you in the head.'*

I stumbled backwards, felt my legs give out from under me, and hit the dirt hard. Brudal had gotten me in the side of the temple with a hammer fist blow. I rolled over backward and got my feet under me. I was seeing stars, but that wasn't so bad; I'd been hit in the head plenty of times lately.

'Not even a real fight,' the big man complained, sneering at the fight master who stood with the cheering audience outside the ring.

I brought my fists up, determined to prove this mountain of gristle wrong about me. That's when I caught the gleam in the fight master's eye and realized his little introduction hadn't been meant to rile up the crowd against me

– it had been meant to manipulate me into fighting *their* way instead of mine.

Clever bastard, I thought.

Brudal looked disappointed, his hopes for a grand, noble victory – something to brag about over beers at the tavern – was looking dimmer by the second. I retreated and watched where his eyes went in the crowd. Was there perhaps a would-be lover among them he'd wanted to impress tonight?

I let myself back up all the way to the ropes as if I were unconsciously trying to run away. Several hands from the crowd shoved me back towards the centre of the ring, right into Brudal's way. His open hand came back to deliver a blow that would've been easy enough to evade, but I didn't; I let him slap me right across the face.

My cheek burned, making it easy enough to conjure tears as I cried out in pain. I stumbled forward – right into a backhand I don't think he'd even meant to deliver except out of reflex.

'My face!' I cried out. 'You broke my cheekbone!'

The crowd couldn't contain their righteous joy at my pathetic whining. The fight master had presented them with a pompous, arrogant woman who used her beauty and cunning as weapons against honest folk. I was giving them the justice they so desired: I wouldn't be nearly so pretty once the fight was over.

Brudal, however, was imagining a different outcome: the one in which his friends spent the next few years mocking his great 'victory' over a hapless woman whose easy defeat had validated all their prejudices. Brudal's gaze went to the flaming red skin of my cheek where he'd struck me, and one arm reached out to steady me in an attempt to convey to everyone watching that, underneath it all, he was a decent guy.

That was his mistake.

I'd used the cheering and roiling of the crowd to give myself the time to plan out each and every step in my mind before I executed them one by one.

The vast terrain of Brudal's body was almost entirely protected from me. His muscles were bigger, his bones thicker. Arms, legs, torso – all of them might as well have been smelted from raw iron. That left only a few precious inches of him that could be conquered. His eyes, for example, were no more durable than mine. The inside of his mouth, his nose, his ears – all as fragile as my own. His neck, well, the muscles were strong, certainly, but not stronger than my legs.

I clamped my fingers around the outside of the wrist on his extended arm and yanked with all my strength. I didn't need to topple him – just tip him enough that he was forced to stick his front foot out for balance. Still holding his arm, I used his bent knee as a stepladder, moving fast as I climbed him like a tree. I wrapped first my left leg and then my right around his neck, and before he knew what was happening, both my thighs were clamped around his neck, cutting off his air.

The crowd brayed their disapproval. Brudal's meaty fingers dug into my calves, unleashing a scream of pain from me. I've been beaten up plenty in the months since I was named a traitor by half the Greatcoats and just about the entire country. A little pain wasn't going to stop me now.

I wrapped my hands around my ankles to tighten my grip and held on like he was the mast of a ship caught in a storm. Brudal's fists began pounding at my shins and knees, but for all his strength, I had the leverage on him. Soon he was stumbling around the ring, searching for the means to shake me, finding no joy whatsoever.

Several among his fellow citizens shouted names at me. I'd heard them all before. A few started hurling stones – most of which struck Brudal instead of me. One left a cut on his forehead that leaked blood into his eyes. For my part, I kept hanging on, squeezing so tightly he couldn't breathe. The setting sun was hitting me full in the face, blinding me, and yet, a profound serenity settled over me.

I hadn't needed to accept this fight. I could've walked away. That's what Falcio would've told me to do. No trial here for me to judge, no verdicts for me to uphold. I wasn't fighting to save someone's life – just fighting because I was sick of people hating me, and of hating myself. More than anything, I was sick of hearing Falcio's voice in my head.

'You betrayed us all,' he'd said to me near the cliffs of Avares after the war had been won thanks to the courage, cunning and daring of the Greatcoats. When he'd walked up to me, I'd almost thought . . . but no, I'd been stupid to think that.

'I'm sorry,' I'd called out to him after he turned away in disgust. 'We . . . He made us believe it was the only way to save the country! Falcio, I'm sor—'

'Don't apologize to me,' he'd said. 'Apologize to the country you betrayed because you thought you knew what was best for them. Apologize to the dead on the battlefield who would still be alive if not for you and the other forty-one Greatcoats who abandoned their oaths.' He'd started walking away from me then. 'Apologize to the King who believed in you when no one else did.'

For the second time, I felt the dusty ground slamming against my back. For a second I feared Brudal had shaken me off, but my thighs were still wrapped around his neck. He tried to get up so he could slam me down again, but even he wasn't that strong. He rolled onto his belly, hoping, I guess, to smother me in the dirt. I tasted sand and muck, didn't much care for it, and kept on squeezing.

Brudal rolled onto his back once more. He was smarter this time, aiming his awkward blows for the vulnerable muscles on the inside of my thighs. A white light of agony burned through me when he got lucky and his knuckles hit the same cluster of nerves Falcio had once chided me for not striking. Despite it all, I kept my hands gripping my ankles so that even as the strength faded from my legs, the pressure on Brudal's neck remained.

'He's done by now,' I thought, feeling him go slack beneath me. I couldn't risk letting him go, though. If he was faking it and I let him free, I'd be done for. Yet, if I held on too long, I would kill him.

This was why Falcio always insisted there were only two kinds of duels: the ones you win at any cost, without hesitation or guilt, and the ones you should never enter into in the first place. Now I was about to either murder a man or become his victim.

The dilemma was solved for me when the crowd rammed past the ropes, yanking the iron posts from the loose ground. Arms grabbed at my ankles and shoulders, dragging me in opposite directions like horses sent to rip me limb from limb. Spittle dribbled onto my cheeks and mouth. When I looked up, the villagers of Phan were in a rage. Before long they were massed on top of me, some punching me with their fists, others holding me down. A couple of them just sat on me, letting their weight force the air from my lungs.

It was a strange sensation: even as I struggled hopelessly to free myself from the swarm of bodies, a part of me couldn't help but concede that I'd spent the better part of my career as a travelling Magistrate searching for justice yet never quite finding it. Since then I had betrayed my oath, lost every friend and comrade I'd ever known, and only here, in this sleepy little village near the desert had I at last found a truly perfect verdict.

This, I thought, as the light from the setting sun faded at last and my eyes fluttered closed. *This is justice.*

3

THE GRAVE

I awoke to the sight of stars overhead and the softness of loose soil underneath my back. What at first I took for a shallow grave turned out to be nothing more than a divot in the dusty grass atop the hill that overlooked the village of Phan.

I wasn't, it seemed, dead yet.

Though I supposed I deserved to be.

No one had forced me into that prizefight. This hill belonged to the villagers, and if they hadn't wanted me coming up here to visit the grave of a dead King, well, I could've just walked away. Hells, I could've waited until nightfall and snuck up here without revealing my presence to anyone. Instead, I'd strode into their village, announced myself and my intentions, and waited for a reaction any fool could have predicted. The Greatcoats had never been popular in these parts, and among the Greatcoats, there was hardly anyone less popular than me these days.

'There's water,' said a voice nearby.

I hadn't heard him breathing, and the ragged, reedy tone made me almost believe – just for a second – that King Paelis had risen from his grave to converse with me. Maybe he would tell me everything was okay, make one of his famously unfunny jokes and, after a suitably dramatic pause, offer me redemption. *'Get off your arse, Murielle de Vierre. This country needs magistrates, even fallen ones, and a King – even a dead one – needs his thorn to stick in the thumb of the unjust.'*

Stupid, the tricks we try to play on ourselves sometimes.

I reached a hand over and traced a line in the dirt until my fingers found the cool metal surface of a tin flask. I unstoppered it and tilted it over my open mouth. The water went down hard and set me to coughing. I'd taken a few blows to the chest that left a deep ache, and from the tightness in my throat, it seemed someone had tried to strangle me after I'd passed out. When at last I deemed myself ready to face whatever unpleasantness still awaited, I propped myself up on an elbow and forced myself to a sitting position. What could've been mistaken for a giant barrel with an oversized cork sticking out the top turned out to be the silhouette of my former – perhaps not-so-former – opponent.

'Funny thing, isn't it?' Brudal asked, sitting at the edge of the hill and looking down at his village below.

'Hilarious,' I replied, rising to my feet. I walked cautiously towards him and nearly stepped on my greatcoat lying on the ground. I guess he'd brought it with him when he'd carried me up here. 'What are we talking about, exactly?'

One burly arm gestured down to the village, the other swung towards me. 'We don't really know ourselves until we meet someone different from us. All the things we think of as familiar, as *natural*, suddenly become foreign.'

It was so like the sort of thing the King might've said – simpler and with less rhetorical flourishes, admittedly, but carrying the same meaning – that for the first time since I'd set off on my journey here, I wondered if perhaps the rumours were true and Falcio really had spoken to the spirit of our dead King upon this hill.

'Are you . . .' Only near-asphyxiation could explain what came out of my mouth next. '. . . my King?'

Brudal laughed, then gagged for a few seconds, finishing it all off with a groan.

'Damn but you have strong thighs, woman. Were you really going to squeeze the life out of me? It's not like I was trying to kill *you*. I thought Greatcoats were all about justice and making the world a little fairer. Here I end up half-dead from you choking me only to then have to fight off my own neighbours to keep them from doing the same to you.'

I couldn't hold back the sinking disappointment that came over me at the way Brudal's words revealed he was nothing more than he appeared, any more than I could deflect the stab of guilt I felt over what I'd nearly done to him.

'I'm sorry,' I said, and despite how tactically unsound a manoeuvre it was, came to sit next to him.

He took the flask back from me. 'Ah, it's fine,' he said

before taking a swig. 'What in the name of Saint Zhagev-who-sings-for-tears was I doing walking into the prize ring with a fighter your size? There weren't many ways you could've taken me down. Should've expected you to try to choke me out like that.'

He rubbed at his neck, which set me to rubbing at my own.

'They're not bad folk,' he went on, still staring down at the village. 'They just . . . they feel betrayed, that's all. Wars come and go, Kings and Queens get crowned and die years or maybe days later, and up here, nothing changes. Harvests are poor at the best of times. We get raided from foreigners to the east and our own neighbours to the west. And every once in a while, someone in a long leather coat stops by and preaches to us about the King's Laws and how everything's going to get better someday soon.'

'I'm not a Greatcoat,' I said. 'I mean, not any m—'

Brutal waived the objection away. 'I heard what you said down in the village. Heard rumours about a bunch of Greatcoats who sided with some arsehole who thought he could put magistrates in charge of the country instead of all these Kings, Duchesses, Margraves, and Daminas. You really bought into that shite?'

'I did,' I admitted. I'd stopped lying to myself on this subject a long time ago. 'I believed every word. Ever since King Paelis died I'd watched my fellow Greatcoats assassinated by petty lordlings all over this miserable country. The very people whose rights we fought and died for spat on us, called us "tatter-cloaks" and blamed us every time their crops failed or some man or woman with a club in hand and a gleam in their eye came raiding. I thought . . . I chose to believe that maybe, if everyone expected us to save the world all by ourselves, well, put us in charge and that's what we'll do.'

Instinctively my arms came up to protect my face, anticipating a violent rebuke over what I'd just said, but Brudal hadn't moved. He just kept sitting there, staring down at his home in the sandy plains below.

'Yeah, guess that makes sense,' he said. 'That why you came north? You figured your King Paelis could give you . . . what's the word?'

'Absolution?'

'I was thinking "redemption", but yeah, absolution sounds right. So, you reckoned some dead King's dried-out bones could give you that?'

I got to my feet and walked over to pick up my great-coat. The leather felt dry to the touch. I hadn't oiled it in months, but the damn thing wouldn't fall apart no matter how I abused it. 'I came here to bury this next to him,' I said.

'What, your coat?' Brutal asked, turning to look up at me.

I nodded.

'What, are you thick or something? Kids come up here to play all the time. One of them would've noticed the upturned earth and dug to find out what was there. A coat this valuable? Somebody would've taken it for sure.'

The thought of an unwary boy or girl fumbling around inside the pockets, skewering their fingers on one of the hidden blades, finding a piece of the hard candy, and ending up beating one of their friends senseless when the effects hit them – or worse, finding the soft candy meant as a last resort against torture . . .

'Hey,' Brudal said, rising to come over to me. 'I didn't mean to . . . Saints, do all Greatcoats cry this easy, or is this another trick to put me off my guard so you can knock me around some more?'

I couldn't hold back the unruly chuckle that came to my lips any more than the sob that followed. When I looked down at my hand, I saw I'd removed the black silk-wrapped piece of the soft candy from the coat. Had that been my real plan all along? Travel five hundred miles to this barren hilltop, bury my greatcoat in an act of petty defiance, and then end it all?

'Did you really think I was King Paelis when you woke up?' Brudal asked. 'I always heard he was a scrawny fellow.'

'You don't look any more like him than I do,' I replied. 'But the King had . . . he had a way with people that's not so different from yours.'

Brudal nodded as if this was somehow the answer he'd expected all along. 'How about, since it's late at night and we're alone up here, the two of us play a little game?' he asked.

'Lay one hand on me and I'll demonstrate the three other ways I could've taken you out that were less pleasant than choking you,' I warned.

Brudal didn't seem the least bit intimidated. 'You're a bit bony for my taste, if I'm being honest. No, what I meant was . . .' he seemed to be reaching for the right words, then finally gave a sheepish smile. 'Those rumours that go around about the dead King's ghost haunting this hill, waiting for his Greatcoats to return . . . how about you and I pretend it's true.' He hunched up his shoulders and stooped in an oddly accurate parody of King Paelis. 'Let's imagine his spirit has taken over my body and he's talking to you through me.'

'I'm not interest—'

'Silence, you impudent tart!' Brudal shouted suddenly. '*This* is how you greet your King? Not with a bent knee – the Gods know I could never convince any of my damnable Greatcoats to kneel before me – but without even so much as a bowed head? Perhaps a "Nice to see you again, Your Majesty"?'

'I . . . Brudal, stop this. It's not—'

The big man put up his hands and turned his head away briefly in disgust. 'Enough of this nonsense, Murielle. You came here to throw away the coat I gave you, to make a mockery of the trust I placed in you. Surely you had words for me as well? Or was I to be spared this sudden disdain with which you treat all I left behind?'

'Words? You want *words*, Your Majesty?' I jabbed Brudal's chest so hard he winced and I feared I might've broken my own finger. 'What did you leave us with but words? A hundred and forty-four different missions given to a hundred and forty-four Greatcoats that made no sense yet somehow you expected us to all fulfill? A puzzle that forms no picture no matter how you arrange the pieces? A riddle with no answer, not even a clever rhyme?'

'Do you remember the words I left you with, Murielle?' Brudal asked.

'Not *words*, "*Your Majesty*". *Word*, singular. One syllable.'

'Then I imagine you haven't forgotten it?'

I started to turn away. However accomplished an amateur actor Brutal was proving to be, I wasn't enjoying this. It hurt me in ways a body shouldn't have to hurt. And yet, I couldn't stop myself from answering.

'Doubt,' I said. 'That's all you gave me that night in Castle Aramor the night before the Ducal army came to take your head. When my turn came and the other Great-coats made way for me to enter the map room and hear your final command to me, all you left me with was, "Doubt".'

'And did you do as I asked, Murielle. Did you doubt?'

I had to unclench my fist just to wipe the stupid tears from my eyes, which then stung from the sand and dirt left behind by the skin from the back of my hand.

'Oh, I doubted, Your Majesty. I doubted everyone and everything, just as you asked. Only, when the misery you left behind got to be too much for me, when one of your own Greatcoats promised me and forty-one others that there was one and only one way to save Tristia, when he preached rebellion and treason and made them sound like loyalty and valour . . . that's when I forgot to doubt.'

There was silence on that little hill a while. I figured even Brudal, committed as he was to this little game he'd devised, couldn't keep up the act any longer. But a person accustomed to the hardships of these lands isn't so easily defeated.

'So you followed my command,' he said finally. 'You doubted me.'

'I told you, I betrayed everyth—'

'You were an imperfect Greatcoat. So what? I was an

imperfect King.' Brudal slapped his hands against his own chest. 'You think this big, moronic lug is any purer a soul just because he's too simple-minded to be otherwise?' His hands clasped together as if in prayer. 'Sometimes a King's schemes demand sacrifice. Sometimes his plans must come within a hair's breadth of catastrophe for victory to be achieved. And sometimes a people must come to the brink of war before they understand the necessity of peace.'

'You're really good at this, you know?'

Brudal ignored me. 'You doubted, and from doubt came betrayal, but there must have been a moment when you realized you were wrong – when the seeming right-eousness of the rebel Greatcoats revealed itself as the first and final step towards tyranny. Do you remember that moment, Murielle?'

I could still put myself there anytime I closed my eyes: standing among Morn's army, alongside Quill and the other Greatcoats who'd committed to his course of action. The cold from the frozen ground on that field near the edge of the mountains had burrowed its way through the soles of my boots like a reprimand from the land itself as I watched that eighteen-year-old girl – Chalmers, they called her, not even a proper Magistrate yet – clothed in an ill-fitting leather coat and riding along our lines, stinking of piss from the fear she held inside even as the Avarean warriors reached out to drag her off her horse and tear her apart.

That moment would never leave me. That girl had shown me what it meant to be a Greatcoat. I'd taken one look at the others, saw in that instant which of them had felt as I did and which, by some inexplicable blindness, still believed we were on the right side. Thirteen of us freed the girl on the horse before the Avareans could kill her. Thirteen of us rode back with her to fight alongside the people we never should've abandoned in the first place. I'd made myself a turncoat twice over.

'Doubt is a painful thing,' Brudal said quietly. 'Not some personal failing, but the first duty of any magistrate.' He placed his hands on my shoulders, and it said something about how confused I was that I allowed him to do so. 'I gave each and every one of my Greatcoats a mission, each one as important as all the others, but the price I asked from some of you was far higher than it should have been. You came to this hill to beg forgiveness of me, I think, but now it is I who must beg it from you. Can you ever forgive me, Murielle de Vierre?'

I broke then – broke like a thin sheet of ice covering a lake whose waters boiled beneath. I was a lost child, falling into Brudal's arms, weeping and sobbing, my fists pounding against his chest. He withstood all of it, the blows and the tears.

An hour must've passed on that hilltop next to a dead King's grave, the ground at my feet watered by sorrows I'd carried with me five hundred miles to reach this soil. When at last I pushed away from Brudal, the big man nodded once, then walked past me to the path that led back down to his village.

'Thank you,' I called out to him. When he didn't stop or turn, I added, 'You'd make a damned fine actor, you know?'

But even that didn't halt his progress, and soon he

faded away into the darkness, leaving me to stare down at the mound where King Paelis was buried, wondering if somehow the scrawny bastard had played one final trick on me.

After a few minutes, I knelt down to pick up my coat, then brushed it off before sliding it over my shoulders and doing up the buttons. When I was done, I set off down the path, not once looking back for any ghostly presence waving me goodbye. Sometimes it doesn't matter whether forgiveness and grace come from a dead King or a town brute.

Sometimes you just need to hear the words.

THE END

MEMORIES OF FLAME

A TALE OF THE GREATCOATS

SEBASTIEN de CASTELL

A MOST TROUBLING TRIAL

To condemn a child is the nightmare of any magistrate, but for Estevar Borros, the King's Crucible, judging the case of a young boy whose mysterious fires have terrorized his entire village risks a sentence worse than death ...

1

MEMORIES OF FLAME

The little boy whistled, and the fire grew. The flames inside the stone hearth danced, though it wasn't immediately apparent to Estevar whether they were responding to the boy's tune or from the wind that snuck in beneath the door and the gaps in the wooden slats that served for windows. Either way, the timber-framed cottage was too hot, and sweat dripped down Estevar's jaw, soaking his elegantly coiffed black beard that was a source of pride to him before sliding down his neck and beneath the collar of his dark crimson leather greatcoat.

The boy wasn't sweating at all.

'Are you here to arrest me?' the boy asked.

'Have you committed a crime?' Estevar asked in return.

Still facing towards the stone fireplace, the boy – Olivier the town constables had said his name was – nodded. Thick ginger curls bobbed up and down. 'I hurt

Jovan Guillet,' he replied. After a moment he added. 'Jovan is my best friend.'

Estevar glanced around the cottage for a chair that might have some hope of taking his admittedly considerable weight. This house was too small, the clay walls too close and the wooden rafters of the roof too low. The conflicting smells of baked bread and unwashed clothes, of rosemary hanging from the kitchen wall and un-emptied chamberpots in the bedroom upstairs burrowed inside his nostrils like earthworms, choking off his breathing.

The flames crackled as if they found humour in his discomfort. Outside, three clerics chanted prayers like braying sheep being slaughtered. Estevar walked the three steps to the wall furthest from the fire and unbuckled the scabbard from his belt so he could ease himself down onto the dusty stone floor.

'Is that sharp?' Olivier asked, turning at last to point at Estevar's rapier.

Settling himself on his buttocks, Estevar drew the weapon from its sheath and held it out flat so the boy could see it. 'This part here,' he said, tapping the thicker steel near the hilt, 'isn't sharp at all, for it must be strong so that it can parry an opponent's attacks and be used as leverage to force their weapon out of the way.' His finger floated up and along to the middle third. 'Here, it is sharper, but only a little, so that the edge may grip and therefore control the enemy's blade.' At last, he came to the narrowest part. 'Now here, where the steel is thinnest, it is weak, but also very sharp. With this, I can cut through hide and flesh with ease. With the tip, I can penetrate thick leather and pierce a body with no more effort than you might put into pushing aside the branch of a sapling.'

Without coming closer, Olivier leaned forward to peer at the rapier, green eyes narrowing to slits. 'Will you stab me with it? If you decide I'm guilty and you have to execute me, I mean.' The boy rubbed at the left side of his chest. 'I don't think I'd like that.'

'I would not willingly choose such an outcome either.'

Outside, the clerics continued their chanting, and though Estevar's study of archaic languages had largely been restricted to legal texts, still he could make out the horrendous curses accompanying their prayers.

Estevar leaned his back against the sandy clay wall, counted to seven as he breathed in, willed his hands and fingers to relax, his heart to stop racing, and slowly released the breath. 'Should neither of us have our way,' he began at last. 'What method of execution would you prefer?'

'Hmm?' the boy mumbled. He'd already turned back to the fire, his earlier question apparently forgotten. 'Do you know where my mother and father are?' he asked.

'Outside.'

'With the priests?'

'Yes.'

Olivier reached up to the mantle above the hearth and took down a small cloth doll fashioned in the shape of a horse. Estevar recalled they gave them as birthing gifts in these parts.

'Is mother cursing me, too?' the boy asked.

'You can understand the language that the clerics are speaking?'

'No, I just . . . they sound very upset. Mother was very upset, too. She was pregnant, you see, and when I came home from playing with Jovan three days ago, she wasn't pregnant anymore. Father said it was my fault. Is that why you came?'

A sudden banging appeared at the cottage door. Three firm thumps of equal force. The rhythm of someone seeking to convey their authority.

Estevar rose to his feet. He did not sheathe his rapier, but carried it openly to the door, and made sure the light caught the blade when he opened up for the constables.

'It's time,' said the master constable, a pair of tiny silver bull's horns on the collar of his heavy grey coat signifying his rank. He was the smallest of the three, but the other two watched him as he spoke, waiting for his signal, rather than concerning themselves with Estevar's bared blade.

'I am not finished,' Estevar told them.

'The priests say it's best done now.'

'The priests can wait.'

One of the other constables sneered but did not speak. This, he left to his superior.

'Listen, Trattari,' the small man said, using the slur for one of the King's order of travelling Magistrates while pulling aside the flap of his coat to reveal the polished wooden stock of a wheellock pistol holstered at his side. It was an expensive weapon, and one Estevar preferred not to contend with. 'You claimed to be some sort of expert in this . . . unnatural business, demanded a chance to talk to it, well now you have, and now it's time to put an end to it.'

It.

How quickly a child's humanity is wiped away.

'A little while longer,' Estevar told them. 'Let me help Olivier understand.'

'Why? What difference would that make?'

'Should you ever be made to suffer the fate you and your priests outside intend for this boy, I suspect such trivial courtesies will mean a great deal to you.'

The master constable gave no response. His eyes never wavered from Estevar's. His right hand though, drew up ever so closely as his fingers reached for the pistol.

Estevar's knuckles rapped against the front of his own dark crimson leather greatcoat. The slender bone plate sewn inside the lining clacked in response. 'Or you can shoot me,' he told the constable. 'And if you are very lucky, the lead ball will pierce my coat and bury itself somewhere permanent, but these coats the King gives us are remarkably durable. I would wager with you that I will survive.' His fingers came up to twist one of the braided and beaded ends of his lustrous black beard. 'Then, my friend, you will face Estevar Valejan Duerisi Borros, the King's Crucible, steel against steel.'

The standoff lasted another few seconds as the wind howled and the priests howled with it and somewhere out there perhaps a kindly Saint howled too at the endless and casual cruelties the world inflicted on children.

'Ten minutes,' the master constable said at last. 'Then we get it done.' He gestured behind himself to Olivier's mother and father, wrapped in blankets against the cold and rain. 'I'll not see them chased from their own home.'

Estevar nodded, and closed the door once again, making sure to slide the bolt back in place.

'Are you trying to save me?' Olivier asked him.

Estevar walked back to where he'd abandoned his scabbard and sheathed his rapier within. He wouldn't need it this night.

'I'm afraid I cannot,' he replied.

The boy looked up at him, his gaze never quite focused on Estevar, as if he couldn't quite tell him apart from the walls or the furniture.

'Well if you aren't here to arrest me or execute me, and you say you can't protect me, then why are you here?'

A fair question – one Estevar had difficulty answering even to himself.

'I am a Magistrate,' he said, and walked over to stand next to Olivier, though not too close. 'One of my jobs is to hear testimony, to weigh evidence, and then to render a verdict.'

Olivier squeezed the little stuffed horse to his chest. 'Is this a trial, then? Am I the defendant?'

'It is a trial, of sorts.'

'And you want to hear my testimony, so you can decide if I'm guilty?'

'I would like for you to tell me about what happened with your friend, Jovan.'

The boy chewed on his lower lip, fingers mashing the soft wool of the horse. Then he nodded to the fireplace. 'Can I show you instead?'

'If you wish.'

The boy knelt down, his face inches from the flames. As he spoke, his breath made them flicker.

'Three nights ago, I was very angry with Jovan because

of what happened when we were playing down by the ravine, so I—'

'What happened when the two of you were playing by the ravine, Olivier?'

The boy turned, and his eyes were no longer green at all but a perfect reflection of the flames in the hearth. 'Don't interrupt me. Jovan interrupted me and it wasn't very nice.'

Estevar put up his hands, to calm the boy, then noticed they were shaking and put them back down. 'As you wish.'

Olivier turned back towards the fire.

'As I was saying, I was very angry with Jovan so I snuck out of the house that night and walked across the field and over the gate into his family's farm. They had a very big farm. The biggest in the valley.'

Olivier blew into the hearth, and the fire seemed to tamp down at first, but then the flames twisted and turned, shaping themselves into red and gold strands, forming the image of a manor house with a barn and several tiny fiery outbuildings.

'I called up to Jovan's window to tell him how angry I was at him, but he wouldn't answer, so I picked up a rock and threw it at his window!'

Suddenly all the miniature windows in the flickering manor house exploded at once.

'I'm a very good thrower,' he said. 'I didn't used to be, but I'm real good now.'

Estevar knelt down alongside the boy, though the heat was brutal, almost smothering. 'Olivier, have you ever known the throw of a single rock to break so many different windows all at once?'

The boy shrugged. 'Maybe it's magic. I can do things now, ever since the accident, I have powers. That's why the priests don't like me. They hate magic.'

'That's very interesting,' Estevar said. He tapped the inlaid design of a cauldron on the left breast of his Greatcoat. 'Do you know why they call me the King's Crucible?'

The boy giggled. 'Because you're so fa—'

'Because I'm the person the King sends to investigate matters that his other Magistrates can't explain. I'm very curious about magic. I'd like to know more about it. Could you tell me how you came by yours?'

But the boy didn't answer.

'The next night,' he said instead, 'I was still angry, so I went back to Jovan's house. I shouted for him, but again he wouldn't answer me. Sometimes he likes to hide in the barn when he knows he's done something bad, so I kicked the barn door.'

Inside the hearth, the flaming barn shuddered, the walls and roof came apart and tiny little flickers that might have been horses and pigs all seemed to flee.

'That must have been some kick,' Estevar observed.

'That was nothing. Last night I was even madder. Why wouldn't Jovan come out and take his punishment like a man?'

'Punishment for what?' Estevar asked.

But the boy wasn't listening to him - perhaps he couldn't hear him at all, not really. He breathed in, deeper and deeper, and suddenly Estevar had to pull up the collar of his coat to keep the chill from his cheeks.

Olivier blew out the air through pursed lips, and the red and gold manor house that had appeared inside the hearth was torn apart by the flames. But still he blew, and embers flew out from the fireplace, and all around the cottage, Estevar was seeing vast fields of barley and wheat, all set ablaze. The flames flickered at the edges of his coat, like wild dogs edging closer to a mountain cat.

'Olivier ...' he said.

'They won't hurt you,' the boy told him. 'I'm not mad at you.'

Estevar tried to keep his tone calm, almost disinterested, so as not to agitate the boy when he asked, 'Are you still mad at Jovan?'

'A little.' Then he lifted his chin and looked up at Estevar. 'Did I kill him?'

Estevar wanted badly to reach out and comfort the boy, but he dared not.

'No, Olivier. Jovan and his family are still alive, but if you were to go back there tonight ...'

Olivier nodded, then did so a second time as if coming to an entirely new conclusion. 'That's why the priests are outside, isn't it? That's why they're trying to damn me – why the constables want you to leave so they can all come inside and perform a ritual against me.'

'They are very worried about Jovan and his family. They're worried, too, about your mother and father.'

Olivier shook his head. 'That wasn't my fault. I was crying, that's all. When I came home three days ago after playing with Jovan, she got very upset. She screamed and screamed. I kept trying to make her stop but I was upset, too, and then ... she started throwing things at me and then it was like her tummy hurt very badly and she ran outside and . . . I was crying, that's all! I just wanted her to hug me!'

'Why?' Estevar asked. 'You seem like a very sturdy boy to me. Why were you crying?'

'Because of what Jovan did down by the ravine.'

'Tell me.'

Suddenly all the flames both real and conjured disappeared, leaving the cottage drenched in shadows. 'No,' Olivier said from the darkness.

Another three knocks came from the other side of the cottage door. Estevar's time was running short.

'Olivier,' he said, drawing his voice from deep in his chest as he did when drawing a courtroom to order. 'Listen to me now. I am a Magistrate, and this is a trial. You are in the dock, and that means you are bound by laws older than the very Gods and Saints themselves. You will render to me your testimony, do you understand?'

Surrounded by darkness, at first, all Estevar could hear was the boy's weeping.

'We were playing,' he said. 'Over by the ravine. Jovan wanted to be the Knight, but it was my turn, so I said he had to be the peasant, but he said his family was rich, and mine poor, so I wouldn't know how to be a Knight.'

The banging became more insistent this time, and the door shuddered against the bolt when someone threw their shoulder into it.

'Go on, Olivier,' Estevar urged the boy.

From the shadows playing about the room, Olivier continued. 'I told Jovan his family might be rich, but nobody liked them because everyone knew they stole the money they used to buy their land. He called me a liar and pushed me. I pushed back, but I'm a lot smaller. We were close to the ledge, and this time when he pushed me…when he pushed me…'

Another thump at the door, different this time. A log perhaps, used as a battering ram.

'What happened next, Olivier?' Estevar asked. 'What happened after Jovan pushed you?'

The flames reappeared in the hearth, not as bright this time, for the room was still cool, almost damp, like wet leaves at the bottom of a ravine. Olivier stood in the shadows, still holding the little woollen horse clutched in his fingers.

'I was so scared,' he said. 'I'd never been that scared. Then something happened.' He took one hand from the horse and tapped his head. 'Here,' he said, then his chest, 'and here.'

Where the boy had touched himself, blood appeared. Thick, gooey blood that drenched his ginger hair and seeped through the linen of his shirt.

'I . . . I was very confused. I ran all the way home because I was so mad at Jovan that I wanted to tell my mother and father what he'd done. I wanted them to hold me and tell me it would be all right.'

The door shook against its hinges, the slat wood frame coming apart around it.

'My father makes an ointment that numbs the pain and keeps wounds from being infected,' Olivier said, oblivious to the constables and the priests coming for him. 'He slathers it on real thick and then you don't hurt anymore. But when I got home, my parents wouldn't look at me. My father yelled over and over, and my mother kept screaming . . .'

This time when the blow came, the door flexed inwards, held there for a fraction of a second as chips of paint and wood flew from its surface, then seemed to almost sigh back into place.

Olivier looked up into Estevar's eyes, and the boy seemed to truly see him for the first time. 'I'm not really magic, am I?'

Estevar Borros, at last, allowed the sorrow he'd kept walled up inside him since he'd been down to the ravine after speaking to Jovan and his family. 'You are . . . a kind of magic, Olivier. But a magic that can't remain here any longer. You need to forgive Jovan, and leave him in peace. You need to let go of your love for your parents, and allow them to grieve.'

The top half of the door caved in. The thick log the three constables were holding retreated backward to prepare for the final blow.

Olivier didn't seem to notice. He was holding up his arm and peering at the slender, bony limb as if trying to see through it. 'I don't feel like a ghost.'

'What do you feel like?' Estevar asked gently.

Olivier opened his mouth to speak, then swallowed, very much as a nervous young boy might do, and for a moment, Estevar could almost make himself believe that this was all some kind of miraculous mistake. Then Olivier's gaze rose back to meet Estevar's once again. 'I think I've been pretending to myself that I'm still here, but I'm . . .' he pressed a hand against his chest as if trying to prove it was there. 'I'm hollow inside. Like a memory that's fading or an echo trapped inside a room that's getting smaller and smaller.'

The boy turned and only now seemed to notice the angry faces of those waiting outside for the wreckage of the door to be cleared away.

'That's why you came, isn't it?' he asked Estevar, gesturing to the priests holding onto their holy symbols, mouthing their words of damnation. 'You want me to go peacefully, but they want to punish me, so you came to help me understand that I died in the ravine days ago and now I'm . . . haunting this place? But what difference does it make to you whether I drift away or am sent to damnation for having burned down Jovan's house and scared people?'

'I am a Magistrate,' Estevar said firmly, determined to keep his voice from breaking. 'The King pays me to see justice done, not cruelty. To me, it means a very great deal what happens next.'

The boy appeared to consider that a moment, then seemed to come to a decision. 'I'll go then, wherever it is one goes after falling down a ravine and smashing one's head and chest on the sharp rocks.'

As the final blow came, the valiant wooden door, at last, gave up its struggle and fell from its hinges to slam against the floor. The master constable entered, his wheel-lock pistol drawn. His two subordinates came alongside, short swords in hand, and behind them, the priests, all save two who were keeping the boy's mother and father from entering.

'Trattari,' the master constable warned.

'Abide,' Estevar said.

Olivier looked at them all, then asked Estevar. 'What happens if after I go the priests decide to perform the rites of damnation over my coffin instead of giving me a proper burial?'

Estevar forced a smile to his face. A bold one. Cavalier – that was the word.

'Ah, to do that, my young friend, they must first face Estevar Valejan Duerisi Borros in the duelling circle, and that would be a . . . grave mistake.'

The boy laughed as he repeated the joke.

He was still laughing as Estevar bent down to kiss the boy's head, his lips feeling only a flickering heat. The fire disappeared from the hearth once again, and the cottage fell back into darkness, all save from the light of the stars shining outside.

Years later, when Estevar was able to overcome his grief and bring himself to return to this place to visit Olivier's grave, the boy's mother told him they had never again been able to keep a fire going in that hearth, and so had to build a second one.

Estevar deemed that as much justice as a world such as this would allow.

THE END

THE ASSASSIN'S HERESY

A TALE OF THE GREATCOATS

SEBASTIEN de CASTELL

PREPARATION IS EVERYTHING . . .

The assassin's true gift is not their talent for killing, but their ability to free themselves from the constrains of morality that enchain even the most shameless murderers. But how does one quiet the voice of one's own conscience at will, and what price does such a talent demand?

1

THE ASSASSIN'S HERESY

I like to remind myself sometimes that I'm not a murderer.

Murderers are amateurs who need only kill their victim once. They rush to do the deed quickly, boldly, because for them, it's the moment that comes after that matters. The murderer dreams of standing over their victim with a bloody dagger in hand, grinning like demon so they may tilt up their chin to the sky as they cry to the gods above, 'See here what I have done? You thought me small, but upon the body of your own creation have I proved you wrong!'

Murderers believe that their crime requires only a steady hand and a fearless heart. We don't care much for hearts in my business, and our hands are always steady. Preparation, though? Preparation is *everything*. Preparation is what reduces the risk of being caught; of being injured; of being discovered. Contrary to all those romantic tales of black-masked rogues whose notorious exploits see them toasted by Viscounts in their parlours and labourers in dusty taverns, no serious assassin ever seeks fame.

We seek . . .

We seek . . .

. . . something else. I don't know what it is exactly, and I'm enough of a professional not to ask myself the more often than necessary. When the question *does* start to pound in my skull, demanding an answer as it does from time to time, I soothe my conscience with preparation.

In the three-foot-high confines of a crawl space beneath a wealthy merchant's villa in the city, I wrestle an emerald gown over my arms and torso, careful not to let the dirt and grime of the floor touch the silk. The odd little red-furred rats that live down here tried to ruin it, but despite their best efforts even they couldn't chew through the leather garment bag I took from upstairs when I stole the dress during out of my nightly visits while the merchant and his family were asleep.

The villa has served me admirably these past weeks, both as a place to sleep in this empty cellar where no one comes and as a source of clothes, makeup, and other supplies for tonight's job. I chose this place in part because the merchant's wife is the same size as I am and has excellent taste. I hope she won't miss the gown too much.

Dressing myself in this dank little crawl space is an awkward, painstaking task. Ah, but life was so much simpler when achieving the peak of fashion and respectability was to slip on one's flea-infested sack dress and crawl out of some dilapidated flophouse to begin the day's begging. Of course, it wasn't all rainbows and puppy dogs; in those days I suffered the jibes, kicks, and occasional attempted rapes of many a fine, upstanding gentleman - and a few ladies, oddly enough.

Maybe that's why I chose this career.

Maybe that's why I started . . .

No. Memories are the past's way of ensnaring us, hunting us down as surely as any constable, seeking to lock us up behind bars harder than iron in a cell from which no one escapes.

I finish dressing: lace collar, undergarments, white gloves. Each item of clothing is another piece of armour that protects me from my enemies and my own unruly conscience. When I'm done, I risk a candle so that I can see myself in the mirror. One of the red-snouted rats tries once more to make its bed in the folds of my gown, but I shoo him away. 'Forgive me, darling, but I'm afraid I need this to make an impression on someone whose company I'll doubtless find less pleasant than your own.'

I glance a final time at the sketch of Aldovar Rego. Dark, curly hair down to his shoulders, a short beard neatly trimmed. And those cheekbones! He's a handsome devil, you have to give him that. But then, aren't all Bardatti Troubadours handsome? All that music and singing isn't what makes them sought after in the ballrooms of Viscounts and Margraves. Yet, there's more to Aldovar than those purely physical attributes the gods gave him. There's something in the line of his mouth, the slight curl of his lip as he grins out at me from the sketch. The Bardatti seem capable of expressions so whimsical and alluring that kings and commoners alike fall under their spell as they sing tales of beloved heroes and daring outlaws alike.

'Keep smiling, Aldovar,' I tell the grinning, square-jawed rogue in the sketch. The thought of killing him - a thought I've moulded and sculpted for weeks now into a careful, intricate, and unstoppable plan - is almost tragic. The juxtaposition of his broad, chiselled, yet somehow elegant and almost feminine features make him the perfect combination of dashing warrior and refined dandy that these Troubadours aspire to be. Looking at the sketch, I want to meet Aldovar, to have him regale me with stories and smiles and kisses. I want to bed him.

But even devilishly charming Bardatti Troubadours can, it seems, piss off the wrong people, and Aldovar Rego has surely done that.

I'm not a murderer, though. I'm not a killer. I'm a weapon: a discreet, infallible, extremely expensive blade. Like all precision instruments, some are finer made and thus more valuable than others.

I'm so expensive, in fact, that you can't buy me. All you can hope for is to rent me for as long as it takes to slit a throat or slide between a pair of ribs to pierce a heart. Like all blades, however, if I weren't available or suited to the job at hand, the customer would simply look elsewhere. If I refused to accept this commission, the man who hired me would find some other weapon. *He's* the murderer, and when Aldovar Rego lies lifeless in a pool of his own blood, it is the client who, from the comfort of his opulent parlour after a succulent meal, sipping a particularly fine glass of wine, will hold the goblet up to the heavens and say, 'See here what I have done, you gods? You thought me small, but upon the body of your own creation have I proved you wrong.'

I'm glad I don't meet the clients. I have a feeling I wouldn't like the kind of person who seeks out my services.

Fortunately, my current *procura homicidus* is by far the best I've ever worked with. The assignments she gets me pay well, but not so well as to attract competition. She never accepts a job without first compiling comprehensive information on both the target and the client so as to ensure there's no funny business going on. They say Gavriel Sanprier of Rijou was close to being the greatest assassin in the entire world until he was sent to murder a Greatcoat named Falcio val Mond. Never accept a job that requires you to kill a legendary sword-fighting magistrate, that's my motto. Best of all though, my current procurator pays a talented portrait artist to produce a sketch of the intended victim so detailed and vivid you could hang it in a gallery and sell it the same day.

One of the rats sits up on its hind legs and tries to chew the paper sketch. I let him have it. I've memorized Aldovar Rego's face, and this is as good a way to get rid of the evidence as any. I watch my little accomplice work for a few moments before removing a set of maschiera paints and brushes from a leather satchel. Sitting cross-legged on a tarp, I begin to create the woman who will set out in high society to find a minstrel of low morals.

As I begin to dab the first brush in the maschiera, I hesitate for a moment. It's more unnerving than you might think to change your face, to become someone else. There's always this moment when you see yourself in the

172 | SEBASTIEN DE CASTELL

mirror as this other person, this human being possessed of a different life and a different set of values. You wonder whether perhaps you might be happier spending the rest of your days in her skin, laughing at the things she finds funny and frowning at those things common to the world that distress her particular soul. Sometimes you look so long into that other face that the thing you want most is to lose yourself, to forget who you once were, and never turn back. *This* is the real risk an assassin of my particular calibre faces; it's not the constables or the courts or the clients, that scares me, but losing myself forever, because the woman I'm pretending to be is a far better one than I am.

I shake that thought away, steel myself, and begin the work with the maschiera paints. The contours of my jaw need softening to evoke youth and innocence. The eyelashes must be longer so they can flutter with ardor when men of prominence honour me with their attention. I use a type of bee venom to swell my lips so that such men won't be able to look at them without desiring to steal a kiss. My nose . . . my nose is fine as it is. Always leave some small part of yourself intact; it lessens the chances of forgetting who and what you are when the moment comes.

I switch to a new brush and a new pallet of maschiera. My skin tone must be darker: a wealthy young woman, still, but one from the country rather than the city. The wig I select is chestnut brown, elegant. I style it in last year's fashion; men prefer women who aren't quite in vogue because they're less threatened by them. They like a girl to possess a certain demure charm, who dresses to please yet is aware that they are less than the other ladies at the party, and thus in dire need of rescue in the form of a gentleman's attention and flattery.

I begin working on the eyes, giving them a wider aspect than my own. This is a lass who is perfectly aware that intrigue and seduction are the favourite sports of the city, but doesn't know how to play those games herself. She's cautious and knows how to handle herself well enough, but she's certainly no duellist, so I relax my shoulders and allow them to roll forward just a fraction. I soften my gaze, make it more furtive and less challenging.

My rat accomplice, having done with Aldovar's sketch, wanders over and props its front legs on my knee, sniffing at me. It's the maschiera paints; they smell a bit like cheese while drying.

'I'm ever so sorry, Master Rat,' I say, then hesitate, adding a tiny stutter to my voice. 'Is it "Lord Rat"? Please forgive me, I should know the proper forms of address, it's just that I'm . . .' I let my eyes flutter downward, awkwardly avoiding the rat's confused gaze. 'I'm rather new to the city and there's ever so much I need to learn.'

No, I think. *'Ever so much' sounds like I'm trying too hard.*

'I'm new to this city and there's a great deal I want to learn.'

Yes. That's better. Less a performance and more an invitation.

I speed up my breathing, making it shallower. The beginnings of a flush come to my cheeks. I do believe the rat is now wondering whether perhaps I'm some sort of mad, two-legged monster come to infect him with rabies.

I pack the rest of the costumes and makeup in the

leather garment bag, and before putting out the candle, I burn the remaining fragments of Aldovar's picture that my rat accomplice has failed to consume. The rat sniffs at my fingers afterwards. Risking a bite and whatever disease might follow, I stroke the fur of his fuzzy little head. He seems to enjoy the attention, pressing his face into my hand and nuzzling my palm. The oddest thought comes to me then: were I myself right now, and not the gentle, innocent, vulnerable young country lady come to naively experience the wonders of the big city, the rat wouldn't take to me so easily - and would, in fact, have bitten me.

I examine myself in the mirror one final time and in that moment; I feel my resolve - the quality on which my profession relies - disappear. I've gone too far this time. The gentle-featured woman in the green dress smiles at me even though I didn't ask her to. Her lips are parting, and I hear her speak to me in a voice that comes from my throat yet isn't mine.

'Were you happier before?' she asks.

'Before what?'

'Before you were me?'

I don't lie - not even for a second. An assassin may deceive the entire world in the course of their work but must never deceive themselves.

'I'm happier now,' I confess to her.

The eyes staring back at me reveal intelligence and curiosity but betray no trace of guile. They are vulnerable, but not passive. When she shifts her hip, just a little, I feel a sensuality inside myself. A desire to feel another's hands on my body, to explore theirs just as thoroughly. The rat nuzzles at me again, wanting me to pet him a little longer.

Even though it's time to leave and my plans require precision, I acquiesce.

'What are you feeling?' the girl in the mirror asks.

I hold up the rat in my hand. 'I like his fur. It's softer than I would've expected and warm. I like the sounds he makes and the rhythm of his heartbeat tapping against my palm.'

'What else?'

'I like that . . . I like that I *like* the rat.'

The girl in the mirror holds up a finger and swivels it back and forth in a slow rhythm. *'Tick tock, tick tock. Isn't it time to go?'*

I set the rat back down on the grubby dirt floor and gently push him away. When I look back in the mirror, the hopeful and happy country girl is gone, and an imposter remains behind, wearing her skin like a cloak against the rain of tears she dares not shed. I have banished this future that isn't mine just as surely as I did the memories that were. When the blade slides across Aldovar Rego's throat tonight, unleashing a torrent of blood down his fine white shirt and blue Troubadour's coat, he won't know it, but *this* was the moment when he died.

A murderer is an amateur who need kill only once. An assassin is a professional who must kill twice, and make of herself the first victim.

See here what I have done, you gods? You thought me small, but upon the body of your own creation have I proved you wrong.

THE END

THE WHEELWRIGHT'S DUEL

A TALE OF THE GREATCOATS

SEBASTIEN de CASTELL

TRIAL BY COMBAT

In the troubled nation of Tristia, trial by combat is no mere rustic tradition but the very foundation of their system of justice. Complex legal rules and convoluted procedures ensure great wealth for advocates and entertainment for audiences.

But not everyone benefits from such laws . . .

1

FIRST BLOOD AND LAST

W hen her time came, the court wardens were forced to drag Janva along the polished marble floor like a squealing calf. The night before, she'd sworn to herself that she would meet her fate with dignity and suffer bravely the hisses of noble Lords and Ladies seated in their scarlet cushioned seats in the gallery above and the jeers and insults of pedlars, minstrels, and even craftspersons like herself from the wooden benches at the back of the duelling court. Janva had failed utterly, and her screams for mercy now echoed throughout the chamber.

No one had prepared her for what it would be like to step inside that massive oval chamber of the Duchy of Luth's Court of Blades, to pass beneath those towering statues of Death and Craft with their cold, unpainted eyes staring down at her without mercy or compassion. Cradled in Death's arm was a huge clock upon which the final minutes of her life ticked away in a relentless drumbeat.

Worse still was Janva's first sight of the six-foot-tall and almost equally wide marble pedestal across the room upon which rested the Magistrate's lustrous oak and silver throne. With his powdered black wig and narrow, colourless face, the man who would oversee Janva's legally sanctioned murder looked like a hunting falcon waiting to leap down from his perch to claw out her eyes.

The thick hands of the court wardens in their black surcoats, grim countenanced, yet with pitying eyes, had been the only things keeping her from collapsing to the floor. One worn shoe now hung off her right foot, the other lost somewhere in the arched passageway that led into the courtroom. The wardens had tried to be gentle with her, but the Duchy of Luth's infamous Court of Blades was no place for kindness.

Three clerks stood behind the Magistrate's throne. One of them, a slender young man with bright, almost playful auburn curls that matched his courtier's smile, stepped down the circular stairs carved into the wide marble column beneath the pedestal to announce, 'Janva Slade, a wheelwright, sentenced to five years for Violence Most Grievous Against a Child.'

Neither the galleries above nor the cheaper rows of benches on the floor were full that day, and those in attendance had clearly paid their visitor's fees in hopes of witnessing more fulsome duels than the one awaiting Janva. On hearing that the victim of her heinous crime was a child, they booed in a sort of weary acquiescence.

Violence Most Grievous Against a Child.

A child? The girl was as cruel a monster as the world had ever spawned. Yet, two days ago, in the Courts Judicial across the street, Janva's testimony against her had been dismissed out of hand by the beatific white-wigged Magistrate. The word of a wheelwright against that of a nobleman's daughter? The verdict had been decided before the case had even been heard.

'Having appealed her sentence with a demand for trial by combat,' the sneering, black-clad clerk continued, 'the accused, Janva Slade-'

Why did he have to keep repeating her name like that - as if she were some notorious child slayer instead of a common craftswoman whose chief crime had been to follow the cries of a terrified boy into the ruins of a broken-down church?

'*Janva Slade*,' the clerk said yet again, pausing for effect as if to draw to himself the attention of the sparse and sullen audience, 'who will this day challenge her sentence in a *duella verdetto* and by steel and whatever mercy the Gods grant her be judged!'

If he'd been hoping to arouse boisterous cheers from the audience, he must've been sorely disappointed by their tepid groans.

Duella verdettos were far from the most exciting events at the Court of Blades, or so Janva's fellow prisoners in the jailhouse had informed her. A prosecuting duellist would be selected - someone the Magistrate had deemed a fair match against the accused - and the two of them would fight to first blood. When Janva lost, as was inevitable given she'd never held a proper weapon in her life never mind a duelling sword, her sentence of five years would be doubled to ten, and that would be that.

Except that Janva had good reason to believe she would never be seeing the inside of a cell again.

'Please!' she shouted, shrugging off the grip of the court wardens who, in their efforts not to injure her before the duel, had loosened their hold on her once they'd gotten her to the defendant's corner. Janva scrambled across the floor, and made it to the base of the massive stone pedestal before they caught up to her. She had to tilt her head all the way back to see up to the Magistrate. 'Please, Your Eminence! They mean to kill me here and now, right before your very eyes!'

That produced more of a reaction from the audience than all the young clerk's theatrical solemnity. Nobles and commoners alike began to laugh out loud. Even the Magistrate chuckled.

'The accused will cease these hysterics, he intoned, readjusting his powdered black wig. His robes were black as well, save for the scarlet bands across his shoulders, and the scarlet hood he would place upon his head when the first duels of the day began. He leaned forward to gaze down at her. 'Your crime, vile as it was, does not warrant a duel to the death. First blood will settle the issue. I suspect it will not be long in coming once the bell is rung.'

'You don't understand!' she cried out. 'In my cell last night, I received a message.'

Quiet murmurs rose up from the audience, enticed by this prospect of illicit goings-on in the jailhouse.

'A message?' the Magistrate asked. 'What sort of message?'

'A single line, your Eminence, a promise of murder to be carried out here in your courtroom. "First blood will be last."'

The murmuring turned to muttering, and then to outright gossiping among the sparse pockets of witnesses spread out across the plush gallery above and the rough wooden benches below. The audience was getting a better show this morning than they'd anticipated. The Magistrate, however, didn't appear pleased by this accusation.

'Produce this note for the court,' he commanded, signalling for one of his other clerks to descend the steps and take it from her.

'I can't,' she replied.

'Why not?' the Magistrate demanded.

She hesitated to answer. What a fool she'd been, to think she might have some chance of persuading him to her side.

'The accused will answer the Magistrate or face remonstration by the wardens,' the auburn-haired clerk declared.

'The message was . . .'

Janva felt her legs give out again and was oddly grateful for the wardens holding her up.

'The message was traced by a finger soaked in soup upon the wooden board beneath my dinner plate, placed there for me to find, the evidence disappearing without any means to preserve it.'

'You mean 'cause you licked up every drop, eh?' shouted someone from the merchant benches.

That set off even more bouts of laughter. The courtroom began to thrum with anticipation. In her vain attempt to elicit sympathy, she'd instead made herself an even more entertaining villainess for them to despise.

'Claims of conspiracy require evidence,' the Magistrate said, bringing quiet back to the courtroom. 'If the accused lacked the courage to enter the duelling circle, she ought not to have demanded the wager of battle for her appeal.'

'It was the only way I could-'

Janva stopped herself. There was no point. She had known the risks when she'd demanded the duella verdetto. She'd not been so foolish as to believe she could win, but a convicted felon awaiting a duel was kept in the city rather than sent straight to prison miles away, and granted visitation rights. Two nights her reckless challenge had bought her. Two nights to spend holding her husband before the wasting disease took him from her forever.

She wished she could still believe those two nights had been worth the price. Ten years in prison was a life sentence to a woman of forty. The message slathered on the wooden dinner tray the night before suggested she wouldn't even have that.

'Please, madam,' whispered one of the burly court wardens as he reached down to lift her up by the shoulder. 'You must retire to the defendant's box while the other cases of the day are called.'

Janva hadn't even realized she'd been on her knees, hands clasped as if in prayer. Who could you possibly pray to in the Court of Blades? The only Gods here were Death and Craft, and neither of them would be on her side.

Even as the wardens led her to the other side of the

courtroom, the clerk began calling the other cases for the day. Janva's duel, though first on the list, would be the third fought. That would give her a little time, an hour perhaps. But time for what?

'Ah, Mistress Slade,' said the heavyset man awaiting her outside the defendants box. He wore a thickly ruffled white shirt and green breeches, all of which he was trying to hastily cover-up behind the black coat he was slipping on over the too-tight white one he'd worn while representing her in the Courts Judicial.

'Advocate Gosse?' she asked, a sudden, desperate hope overwhelming her instinctive dislike for the man. He'd taken every penny she had to mount her defense, if such a lazy bout of speechifying could rise to the level of a defense. 'Have you found some grounds to appeal-'

'What?' His lip curled below his thin grey moustache, revealing he held her in no higher regard than she viewed him. 'No, of course not. I told you two days ago, once you issue a demand for an appeal by combat, there can be no further legal maneuverings.'

'Then why are you here?'

He smiled and finished buttoning up the black coat required of advocates in the Court of Blades. 'His Eminence the Magistrate *did* grant my one small appeal. I am to act as your duelling *advisoro*. No charge to you, either! The court itself will cover my fee to ensure fair justice today.'

'You're to be my second?' she asked. 'My-'

'No, madam,' he said, putting his hands on her arms as if she were becoming hysterical. He'd done that to her a half dozen times during the trial, too. 'Alas, the judge would never approve of another fighting in your stead. No, my role today is to advise you on how best to approach the coming duel.' Effortlessly, his arm slid across her shoulders as he pointed with his other hand to a pair of rough-looking men in their thirties standing at opposite sides of the duelling circle as men in dark robes handed them their respective duelling swords. 'Now, there are two other duels before yours. I recommend you watch how the gentlemen involved handle themselves prior to and during the fight. That way you're less likely to embarrass yourself before the court.'

'Embarrass— Gosse, didn't you hear me before? Whoever the Magistrate has designated to duel me is planning to kill me in there! Can't you-'

'As to that . . .' he said, interrupting her as he reached a hand into his coat and pulled out a folded note. 'It appears your opponent is to be the girl's brother. He made an appeal *ab calamitas* to be allowed to champion his family's honour.'

Gosse put the note away and squinted across the room towards the prosecuting duellists box. 'Ah, there he is. Praezan, I believe he's called. Handsome fellow, wouldn't you say?'

Janva's fists clenched and she had to fight not to elbow her *'advisoro'* in his ample belly to get him away from her. Even this much satisfaction she was denied, however; he was the only person in this courtroom even nominally on her side.

Praezan Cuvier looked to be about twenty-five years of age. Tall and long-limbed, she noted. He shared much of his younger sister's features: straight blond hair that fell to his collar, piercing green eyes and a thin, cold smile as he caught her staring at him. He had his sister's bright complexion and high cheekbones as well, though Janva supposed the girl's face no longer resembled what it once had.

I had no choice! Janva told herself, just as she'd pled to the Courts Judicial during her trial. *What she and the other girl were doing to that boy . . . it wasn't right! It was-*

'There, see?' Gosse said, his arm having dropped to her waist and now squeezing her tight to him as he pointed to the two men who'd begun the duel. 'Watch and learn, my dear. Keep your distance as best you can; don't try to get in too close. Arm fully extended - that's important. And when the weapons masters offer you a choice of swords, take one of the slender ones. They're sharper and will better suit the limited strength of your arm.'

'Now *that* is excellent advice,' said a voice behind them, deeper than Gosse's, yet flat and cold as the crackling surface of the ice over a lake in winter. That voice made her shudder. 'Assuming, of course, that what you want is to die from a rapier blade driven into your intestines.'

Janva turned, momentarily relieved to have an excuse to get away from Gosse's clutches without risking offence. The man who'd spoken was of middling height, perhaps an inch or two taller than her. He was neither thin nor heavy, but somewhere in between. His hair was cut short, given no particular style. His face would have been handsome had he lent any expression to his features whatsoever. He wore a long, dark brown leather coat, and kept one hand in his pocket. The other hung at his side, the fingers moving with tremendous speed, tapping against each other in a sequence as if he were playing a melody on a flute.

'Who are you?' she asked.

'Yes,' intervened Gosse as he pushed her aside to press his belly against the other man. 'Who do you think you are to interrupt an advocate counselling his client.' He poked a finger against the other man's chest. 'One word from me and the wardens will have you in irons, sir! Now tell me your name so I may ensure it is correctly spelled upon the judicial complaint.'

Whether the man found Gosse's attempts at intimidation frightening or amusing, Janva couldn't say, for his expression didn't change. He might've been drunk, or asleep, or simply deaf and hadn't heard the threat. The only thing about him that moved at all were his fingers, tapping against one another in that endless rhythm.

'Call me Ache,' he said at last.

'What?' Now Gosse grabbed the other man by the collar. 'Play no games with me, sir!'

Again the man made no move against Gosse, merely said impassively, 'I am the ache in your fingers on cold winter nights. I am the ink scrawl on every legal document you attempt to write and the fumbling of wine goblets and teacups at your dinner parties. I am a lifetime of regret should you fail to remove your hand from me, turn around, and leave this courtroom immediately.'

To say those things, to say them without emotion, without inflection, without even malice, was a terrifying thing to behold.

'What do you want with me?' Janva asked.

Even now he didn't bother looking at her. His gaze was across the courtroom, focused, she was convinced, upon Praezan Curvier in the prosecuting duellists box. 'I would like to offer you a little advice,' he said. Now his eyes shifted fractionally, coming to rest on Gosse's hand upon the collar of his leather coat. 'Once my present business is dealt with.'

Gosse looked down, too, and like Janva no doubt wondered what the hand hidden in the pocket of his coat was holding.

'As you will it,' the advocate said at last, releasing his hold on the other man's collar and spinning on his heel. 'The advisoro fee was negligible anyway, and I am well rid of this case.' He took three steps towards the aisle that led out of the courtroom before pausing to look back at her, lips twisting into an expression of disgust. 'You deserve to die for what you did to that girl.' His smile returned, and Janva recoiled before her former advocate's gleeful malevolence. 'First blood will be last.'

2

CRUELTIES

Before Janva could interrogate the mysterious man in the long brown greatcoat who'd referred to himself 'Ache' and had terrified away her advocate on what, precisely, he'd meant by offering her 'a little advice', he began peppering her with questions.

'The men facing each other in the *duella civitas*,' he said, pointing to the duelling circle. 'What can you glean from their fight?'

It struck her as odd that his first act after ejecting her previous advisoro was to instruct her to do the exact same thing Gosse had told her to do. Although, Ache seemed less interested in telling her what to think than asking her opinion.

Janva turned and watched the opponents, quietly relaying what she saw so as not to attract any unwanted attention. 'They're both young and fit,' she began, reaching for whatever observations sounded remotely sensible.

'They appear almost equally skilled, though the taller one is more aggressive.'

The more she watched, the more in awe she became of this vicious and yet elegant form of combat. 'Their blades almost dance in the air,' she went on. 'Their steps are light, as if the two of them are skipping from rock to rock across a raging river. There's a music to the way their swords clash against one another, a rhythm a . . . melody.'

She glanced back at Ache, who himself was so quiet that she fairly expected to find him gone.

'Well?' she asked.

'You've seen nothing,' he informed her, his right hand still buried in his pocket.

Despite the surge of resentment she felt at his glib dismissal, tears came to Janva's eyes. 'I'm minutes from being handed a sword and sent to die in that circle, and that's as much compassion as you can muster for me? Who are you working for, "Ache"? What is your purpose coming here?'

He gave no answer, not to *her* questions at any rate.

'In the mere moments I gave you to examine the duel, there was only one thing you could possibly learn of importance.'

Janva wiped the dirty sleeve of her linen shirt across her eyes. 'What, then?' she demanded. 'What is this magnificent insight a wheelwright was supposed to learn glancing at two trained sword fighters for a few seconds?'

Finally, he seemed to look at her, but there was nothing reassuring about his attentions. 'You aren't them, Janva Slade. They are young where your best fighting years passed you by a decade ago. They are slender of build and light on their feet. You're thick-bodied. Even standing still I can tell you're slow of movement and reflex. You have no training, no experience, and no confidence - which is the most useful duelling skill you possess from what I've observed thus far.'

This time she couldn't stop herself from crying out, but the audience was so enraptured by the duel no one seemed to notice. 'You think I don't know these things? You think my wits are as thick as you deem my body? Are you really so callous as to come mock a besieged, middle-aged craftswoman who will never know old age?'

Ache seemed to absorb her words slowly, as if they came out of a tall glass from which he took one small sip at a time.

'I could weep for you, if you wish,' he said after a time. 'In fact, no- let me promise you this much. If you die here today, Janva Slade, I'll see to it personally that you're buried in a proper grave in the city cemetery. No pauper's ditch for you. I'll visit your friends and loved ones who couldn't afford to pay the visitor's fees to witness your trial, and speak to them of your valour and courage. I'll serve as one of your coffin bearers, and offer a eulogy at your funeral. And when the last shovelful of dirt falls upon your casket, then, madam, I will weep for you. Does that ease your suffering?'

Janva wasn't stupid. She'd dealt with disdainful men and women her whole life, from her teachers at school to the master wheelwright under whom she'd apprenticed - and who'd made her pay double the fees for the privilege. She'd negotiated with merchant princes and gangs of thugs. Janva knew contempt and ridicule even when it came without the slightest smirk or sneer. Ache didn't seem to be mocking her.

'Thank you,' she said, barely audible over the sudden cheers as the first duel ended with a shoulder wound on the shorter man, followed by the court wardens ushering them out of the circle so the next case could be fought. 'Those things you offered . . . if you will honour those promises to me, they will make my passage into death easier today.'

Ache returned her gaze, his dark brown eyes narrowing. 'Then I rescind them all.'

'What?'

'I take it all back. Not one of those things will I do for you, Janva Slade. Your death will be miserable. Pathetic.' He nodded towards the common benches at the back of the courtroom. 'I'll pay silver to one of the minstrels here to compose a comedic song about the lowly wheelwright who beat an innocent girl near to death only to wet herself when she faced her own. I'll see to it th-'

'Stop!' Janva shouted at him, pounding a fist against his chest. Beneath the leather of his coat was something hard, like a steel plate, and it hurt her hand, making her even more miserable and outraged. 'No more of your foul words! Leave me to my dying, you soulless bastard! You call yourself Ache, but I know your true name now, even if your own mother didn't. You are Cruelty! Do you hear me? Cruelty itself!'

Two dozen hushing voices reprimanded her. The Magistrate slammed his sceptre down on the brass bell mounted on the arm of his throne. The two court wardens in their black surcoats approached them. Ache waved them away, and for no reason Janva could imagine, they turned and walked away again.

'Why did those men obey you?'

'I did them a favour once,' Ache replied. 'In exchange, when I come through these parts, they provide me information on such matters that might interest me.'

'What matters?' Janva asked.

As seemed to be his habit, he ignored the question.

'Why did you do it, anyway?' he asked her. 'The girls in the church. There were two of them armed with foot-long fighting daggers - though I note that was left out of the court records.' His eyes met hers and he repeated his question. 'Why didn't you leave well enough alone?'

Janva was taken aback, and even as the next duellists entered the circle - two women this time, though young and fierce and as unlike her as the men previous had been. They reminded her of the two girls, in a way, which made Janva shudder.

When she'd heard those screams . . . the boy had sounded like a cornered animal, almost braying more than crying. Janva had never heard anything so awful, so heart-rending. And then to walk into that abandoned church, to see those two girls- No, young women! Fourteen at least, dressed in expensive coats and riding trousers. The boy was a pauper's child in near rags. They'd tied his arms to one of the pews, his ankles spread out and bound to a three-foot length of wood, flat on his belly with his trousers gone. His bottom was covered in welts from their riding crops, but that had only been the beginning. When Janva had come into the church, the girls

were giggling, and the older one - the Cuvier girl - was . . .
she... was . . .

'When I'd chased off the younger girl,' Janva said, her
voice ragged, almost wheezing as if she were having
trouble finding her breath, 'the other one was about to
leave as well. She . . . she almost sauntered away from me.
Then she said, "we'll only find him again tomorrow. Or
maybe someone else." And then she'd looked up at me
and smiled so brightly. "Do you have a son?" she asked.'

Janva shook her head as if doing so would drive that
smile, those words, from her mind. She didn't have a child
of her own. Her husband's disease— Yet the way the girl
had spoken to her, so filled with glee . . . 'I didn't mean to
hit her so hard,' she whispered.

'You broke the top right corner of her cheekbone with
the handle of your wood auger,' Ache said dispassionately.
'The blow was so hard her neck wrenched to the right.
When she fell, the back of her skull cracked on one of the
stones from the broken roof.'

'I didn't mean-'

'You struck the blow. I bribed her physician for information. She'll recover, though she'll never be as beautiful
as her parents hoped. The cheekbone will forever sag, and
the scar across her face will never go away. You've taken a
great deal from her. I wonder, though, if you could go
back, would you perhaps walk past that church?'

A scream from the duelling circle made Janva turn. At
first, it seemed as if one of the women had suffered a
mortal wound, but it proved to be a shallow cut. The
Magistrate halted the fight and asked if she yielded. Her
grin gave him the answer, and the duel resumed.

'Yes,' Janva said, turning back to Ache. 'I would live free so that I could be with my husband in his final days. I would walk right past that church and . . ' She stopped, unable to keep the lie going. 'No, damn you. I would do it all again, though perhaps I'd try not to hit her so hard. What she was doing to that poor boy . . .'

'We'll only find him again tomorrow.'

'That "poor boy" you speak of testified against you in court,' Ache reminded her. 'He told the Magistrate of the Courts Judicial that he was a willing participant in the girls' games. I understand his family received a tidy sum for his brave testimony.'

'Not his fault,' Janva insisted. 'What they were doing - it's hard for a boy to adm-'

'May the lad burn in whichever hell will have him,' Ache said casually.

'What?'

'He was helpless, begging, we can assume, for someone to save him. You risked your life and your freedom for him. In return, he lied so that you would rot in prison. This is not the means by which we achieve a fairer society.'

Before Janva could counter that whatever society he dreamed of had never existed and never would, a polite cough from close behind made her turn. Two weapons masters in black robes bore a set of black lacquer cases in their arms. When Janva looked past their shoulders, she saw the second duel was done, and Praezan Cuvier was taking a few swipes in the air from the edge of the duelling circle with a long-bladed rapier. He followed these up with a few lunges in which he stamped his front foot very hard and shouted, 'hah!' as his blade struck what Janva was sure was meant to be her heart.

'Amateur,' Ache observed.

'Madam,' said one of the weapons masters. 'We have eight choices for you today. My colleague will begin with the lightest, which is also the sharpest.'

The second man began to open a case, but Ache leaned past Janva and snatched one of the cases with his left hand, then rested it on his right arm. After snapping open the latches, he gave it a cursory glance before removing it from its black velvet nest.

'This one,' he said to Janva, handing it to her.

'You . . .' breathed one of the weapons masters. His eyes were locked on Ache's right arm - or rather where it ended.

All this time, Janva had thought he must be holding some weapon in his pocket - perhaps an illicit stiletto or blinding powder he meant to offer her to use against Praezan. But now she saw why he kept his right hand hidden: because he didn't have one.

The weapons masters looked as if they might summon the wardens or perhaps simply run screaming. 'You have no jurisdiction here, Greatcoat,' one of them said to Ache. Janva had the impression he was being terribly brave doing so.

'I'm fully aware that the Duchy of Luth has banned the King's Travelling Magistrates from taking cases in these lands,' Ache admitted. 'I am merely here to provide counsel to the defendant on certain matters pertaining to the finer points of swordplay.'

Without another word, without even verifying if Janva

was agreeing to the sword Ache had selected for her, the two weapons masters scurried away.

'This court will be in recess for ten minutes by Death's clock,' said the Magistrate with a single clang from his sceptre on the bell by his throne. He rose wearily to begin his descent down the winding steps carved into his massive pedestal. 'After which the duel of Praezan Cuvier versus Janva Slade will begin.'

'What happens now?' she asked Ache, no longer sure what to think, who to believe, or what in the world she was going to do when she stepped into that duelling circle with a man nearly twenty years her junior and twice her size. 'Who are you, really?' she asked then, grabbing hold of his right sleeve and staring at the stump of his missing hand. 'What is your purpose in coming here today?'

With his left hand, he took the rapier from her, then made her extend her arms so he could lay it across them and examine the blade's straightness and balance.

'Three questions you've asked, so three I'll answer,' he replied, bending down to peer at the curving bands of steel sweeping around the hilt's quillions. 'In reverse order, my purpose today is to see justice done in a Duchy that has, so far as I can glean, abandoned it recently. As for my name, I am Kest Murrowson, once called the King's Blade.' He held up the stump of his right arm. 'Contrary to appearances, and with, I assure you, neither arrogance nor modesty, I am the single greatest expert on the art of the sword who has ever lived.'

Janva nodded to his missing hand. 'Looks like you lost at least one fight.'

It was a glib remark, and more callous than she

intended, but Ache . . . Kest, rather, took it entirely seriously. 'No, madam, I have never lost a swordfight. It is merely that, unlike many in this country but not, I suspect yourself, I know that not all victories come without cost.'

Janva had never given much thought to victories. They weren't part of a wheelwright's life. But then she recalled that brief moment after she'd knocked down the Cuvier girl and freed the boy, felt his skinny arms grab around her waist as he wept with gratitude even before he pulled his pants up. That had felt like a victory. And surely she knew now it had come at a cost.

'What now?' Janva asked, repeating her earlier question. Barely thirty yards away, Praezan Cuvier stood outside the duelling circle, waiting for the Magistrate to return so he could avenge the assault on his young sister. He probably felt like a hero right now.

Ache - for she decided that name suited him better than 'Kest' - reached out with his left hand, gently took her chin, and turned her head towards him. 'Now I teach you three things. Three simple truths that you will use to violate every comforting belief the people in this courtroom hold about you, about the world, and most of all, about duelling.'

For the first time, he gave her a smile. He wasn't very good at it.

'Listen closely, Janva Slade, for this is how you're going to win.'

A SINGLE TICK OF THE CLOCK

J anva shook as she moved in halting steps around the duelling circle. Her feet felt heavy, the rapier Ache had selected for her - far too long for her body - leaden in her arms. Her posture was ridiculous. Even *she* knew a proper guard had you presenting the narrowest possible target by keeping your sword arm side to your opponent, arm three-quarters outstretched. You could see people doing so in open-air fencing halls all over the city. It was basic science: a smaller target with longer reach means better form.

Janva, on the other hand, was leading with her left shoulder even though her rapier was in her right hand. She was resting the blade on her left forearm, which less-ened the weight on her sword arm, but meant she was presenting a foreshortened weapon. She was also hunched down, her shoulders practically up around her ears. She must've looked like an idiot.

Praezan watched her quizzically as he circled her,

forcing her to keep shifting her weight to keep him from flanking her. He moved like a cat. A damned *cat*.

'*His first mistake was sending you that message,*' Ache had told her before the Magistrate had returned to gavel the commencement of the duel. '*First blood will be last is a fine turn of phrase, but it also puts him in a box.*'

'*I'm fairly sure I'm the one who's going to end up in a box,*' she'd reminded him.

'*He can't afford a glancing blow, don't you see? He needs to pierce you through the heart, the stomach, one of the other organs, or through the throat. Even the eye is unlikely to kill you given the court must provide medical assistance at the end of the duel.*'

How reassuring, she'd thought, but she wasn't stupid either, and whatever chance she had of survival was dependent on gambling that this enigmatic man was half as good as he claimed.

Praezan gave a tentative thrust to Janva's left side. She closed her eyes.

'*Seriously?*' she'd asked. '*You want me to close my eyes when he attacks?*'

Ache had been merciless in his analysis. '*You're too slow to avoid a lunge and not skilled or strong enough to parry one. So what difference does it make if you see it coming or not? Better that you don't overreact to it by lurching backwards and falling over your own feet.*'

Whatever genius this man possessed in the arts of duelling, Janva was fairly sure he'd have made an absolutely terrible fencing instructor.

Praezan lunged at her, again aiming off by just a hair to get her to open up and try to parry. When she didn't, he turned the blade of his rapier a quarter turn and smashed her leg with the flat. No blood, so the fight continued, but now her knee was screaming in pain and she was limping.

'What happens when he doesn't feint but instead tries to stab me?' she'd asked then. The answer to that had been perhaps the only time Ache had shown her any real compassion.

'What's the worst pain you've ever known?' he'd asked her.

'Watching my husband wasting away no matter how hard I-'

'Of the body, not the heart. Your heart won't do you any good in the duelling circle, I promise you.'

She hadn't had to think hard to come up with the answer he was looking for. *'A carriage whose wheel I was replacing tipped over on me. The merchant who owned it had insisted on not paying for extra labour and assisted me himself, but he failed to put the blocks underneath properly.'* Janva had shown Ache her left shoulder which still hung lower than the right because it had never fully healed.

'Does it still hurt?' he'd asked, squeezing it with his left hand - Saints but the man was strong - until she'd nearly cried out.

'Yes, damn it!'

'Good,' he'd replied. *'That's good. Another advantage over your opponent.'*

'How? He looks like he's in perfect condition. Probably never broken a bone in his life.'

'Exactly. He's never known agony, likely never known the despair or the overwhelming urge to curl up when it comes. Tell me, when the carriage fell on you, did you freeze up?'

A small surge of pride there. *'No, I took the weight on my broken shoulder so I could reach out with my free hand and piled the blocks back up beneath the side of the carriage so that I could then turn without it crushing me.'*

Ache had released her shoulder then. *'Then here at last is some semblance of justice. That carriage that broke your shoulder is about to save your life.'*

'How?'

And then he'd explained the plan to her.

May every God and Saint damn the man, his scheme was simple, terrifying, and without doubt the only chance she had.

The crowds had grown in the hour since she'd first been dragged into the courtroom by the wardens. Evidently, those in attendance had run outside during the recess and let passersby know that today's duella verdetto was going to be more entertaining than people assumed. Those they'd convinced to come and pay the visitor's fees were no doubt suitably irritated by now.

'Stop waddling about you fat duckling!' a man in minstrel's blues shouted from the cheap seats.

One of the nobles from the gallery threw something at her. A piece of cake. Some of it hit her face before landing on the polished wooden floor. Janva licked her lips. Delicious.

'Halt!' the Magistrate called out.

She didn't, though, and neither did Praezan. Even as the Magistrate scolded the audience, they kept circling.

I can see you now, she thought, watching him. *You mean to kill me. You don't even care if the Magistrate figures out it was intentional. You know he won't have you prosecuted.*

Praezan smiled at her as if he could read her thoughts.

She supposed they weren't hard to guess given her teeth were chattering from fear.

Been afraid plenty of times, she thought. *All those nights with the man I love, watching him waste away and wondering how I would live without him. This isn't so bad by comparison.*

'Come on,' Praezan cooed to her. 'Show us how you beat up little girls. Show us the monster you hide behind that weepy, pathetic, slack-jawed face of yours!'

Now she felt a stab of fear, for this was the cue. This was what her supposed genius advisoro had told her would be the moment.

'When he calls you names, he'll be trying to goad you into attacking, but that will reveal that he's growing frustrated and desperate. In his attempt to lure you out, he'll be hiding his own reckless urges.'

'So you want me to insult him back?'

Ache - Kest, actually, because in that moment he really did look like some gallant travelling Magistrate - said, *'No, in full payment for the service I have rendered you, you will say these words as I give them to you now.'*

So Janva, still presenting her left side to him, still scrunched down and bent over like a hunchback, said the words.

'By the laws of this nation, not the petty rules of this Duchy but the King's Laws themselves, I do hereby declare that your sister, Tanliza Cuvier, did viciously and with malice violate a young boy, and so long as I draw breath, I will not rest until she is prosecuted for her crimes.'

There was a sudden hush from the audience. No one had expected to hear such a thing from some stoop-backed wheelwright in the middle of a duel in the Court of Blades. The Magistrate rose up, furious that anyone would dare to suggest the King's Laws still had sway over those of the Duchy of Luth. He smashed down his sceptre upon the bell, and the clang rang out through the courtroom, but no one paid attention, least of all Praezan Cuvier.

'It will all happen fast,' the Greatcoat had told her. *'But it will seem slow. Nothing fancy, merely a single, simple move performed under the worst circumstances imaginable.'*

Praezan's shock registered on his face. He must've truly loved his sister, for to hear her slandered this way with such . . . formality from someone so lowly as Janva seemed to drive him almost mad in that moment. The need to hurt her - to make her pay - overcame his scheme to kill her on first blood.

Kest had told Janva that it would be all right to close her eyes for the blow, but she didn't. She wanted to see it coming. Even before he lunged at her, she ground her right foot to the floor. The target she offered was her left side, her hand and forearm up to cover her face. Praezan was nearly a foot taller than her, which meant in his furious, uncontrolled lunge, the point of impact became predictable. Behind her hand, Janva saw the tip of his rapier fly towards her, then felt it bury itself deep in her shoulder.

She'd assumed the pain would be even worse than the horse cart that had once fallen on that same shoulder. Yet, all she felt was a dull, sickening thud as the point of Praezan's rapier struck the bone, almost as if he'd punched her with his fist.

Remember the movement, she started to tell herself, but by then it was all over. Kest had been right, though: it *had* seemed to happen slowly.

As the rapier's point pierced cloth, skin, and muscle to then push into the bone of her shoulder, her rooted right foot caused her to pivot like a weather vane caught in a sudden gust of wind. Her body turned counter-clockwise, and with all the strength she possessed, she extended her right arm, and with it, the tip of her own rapier.

'Two and a half pounds of pressure,' the Greatcoat had informed her. *'The opponent maybe twice your size or half your age, but two and a half pounds of pressure is all it takes for a sharpened rapier blade to pierce flesh.'*

Another detail on which his expertise was now well proven.

Janva watched almost as if from a distance as her point breached Praezan's leather duelling vest. Kest had warned her that a rapier blade needed less than three pounds of force to penetrate leather and flesh, and Janva had a wheelwright's strength and precision. Still, she would've expected some resistance - some tiny moment of delay when the tip struck the outer layer of her opponent's vest or the youthful muscle beneath. But not even a fraction of a second passed between that first kiss of steel and the blade burying itself six inches into Praezan's chest.

From chaos to utter silence. No one spoke, no one seemed even to breathe. For that one instant, not a single noise could be heard in the Court of Blades ...

... only the quiet ticking of the great clock held in the arms of the statue of the God of Death as he and the God of Craft watched the proceedings with sublime disinterest.

Praezan's eyes were wide, but he wasn't looking at the sword in his chest, nor his slender blade still caught in Janva's shoulder, bent into an arc when she'd twisted a quarter turn counter-clockwise to face him. Praezan was looking into Janva's eyes.

'Guilty,' he said before he fell.

4

THE POINTY END
FIRST BLOOD WILL BE LAST.

Praezan Cuvier had made good on that threat,
delivered by a corrupt jailor in a smear of soup on a
wooden tray. His promise had not, however, been fulfilled
in the manner he'd hoped. Both Praezan's thrust and
Janva's counter had, in accordance with the traditions of
the Court of Blades, taken place in the same tick of the
clock cradled in the stony arm of the statue of Death.
Thus the two blows were deemed simultaneous and
weighed against each other to determine guilt. His had
drawn blood, hers had ended his life.

The problem with winning one of the most unexpected victories in the history of the Court of Blades was
that not everyone was keen to accept it. Praezan had, it
turned out, a number of friends in attendance. They,
being brave and stout souls, took it upon themselves to
finish what their comrade had begun.

Janva had turned to Kest, assuming this so-called

legend of the sword would leap into action to save her. He hadn't, though; it was the court wardens. Though they were far more compassionate souls than she would've believed even yesterday, in truth, they had little toleration for violations of court procedure.

Soon, order was restored. A half-dozen of Praezan's supporters were in irons for their attempt to overthrow the court's authority. The nobles in the gallery and the common folk in the benches had settled down, and the Magistrate had come out from behind his throne.

Janva, her bandaged shoulder so covered in narcotic salves she nearly giggled through the end of the proceedings, had the unique pleasure of watching His Eminence stutter out his new finding of not guilty by evidence demonstrated through trial by combat.

'So it's over then?' she asked Kest as they finally left the courthouse.

'Legally, yes,' he said.

That answer didn't reassure her.

'You mean they might come after me through other means?'

He surprised her though with an almost bewildered shake of his head.

'Janva, I think you'll find the Curvier family's fortunes will wane somewhat in this city. The people of Tristia have a strange obsession with trial by combat. It's as close to a national religion as we have. I suspect you'll be left alone from now on, though perhaps you'll notice a wealthier clientele for your business.'

The two of them walked in silence down the streets. It

took nearly an hour to reach her home and she was barely able to stand by the time they arrived. Kest had insisted it was better this way, though: sometimes it takes a great many miles to leave the violence behind you and not bring it back to those you love.

'You're not coming in?' she asked when he started to turn away from her door. 'I want my husband to meet the man who-'

Kest held up both his hands - including the missing one. 'I offered you a little advice, nothing more.'

'I thought you said you weren't one for false modesty. You saved my life.'

He came closer then and put his left hand on her good shoulder. 'It's as I told you before - I am neither modest nor arrogant. Listen close now, Janva Slade, because I never waste my time with idle praise. Not one in a hundred people could do what you did today. You faced death and withstood agony without flinching. The same spirit that made you step into that church when you knew you should've walked on by is the one that allowed you to win the duel today.' He leaned over and kissed her forehead. 'On behalf of a dead King and a dream still living, I thank you.'

'For what?' she asked hastily, because she was finding herself oddly tempted to cry now.

This time when he smiled, it seemed more genuine than the one before, almost like a young boy gazing up in wonder at the stars on a clear night. 'For reminding me that justice is not so far out of reach as it sometimes seems.'

As he turned to go, she found herself unexpectedly asking, 'These Greatcoats of yours . . . I assume they're mostly young folks. Trained in swordplay and duelling and the law and such?'

Again he became still, as he'd been when first she'd met him in the courtroom barely two hours before. 'For the most part. It's a difficult job.'

Janva bit her lip, decided not to press the issue, but then, foolishly, heard herself ask, 'Then I guess they haven't much use for middle-aged wheelwrights who barely reads and only recently learned which end of a sword is the pointy one?'

Too late, she tried to paste a wry smile over her features to mask the terrible earnestness with which she'd asked the question. She'd hoped he might smile tolerantly in response, or share a laugh at such a preposterous idea. But even in the short time of their acquaintance she'd concluded that Kest wasn't one for frivolity. This was a man for life and death were matters of mathematics, and in such equations pity was a futile – even dangerous – diversion.

He gestured towards the trade road. 'Three hundred miles to the west, as the crow flies, lies Castle Aramor.' He nodded to her door. 'When your husband's time has come, when the grieving wearies you and you begin to wonder whether perhaps the world might do well to be just a little bit fairer, make your way to Aramor.' His left hand tore one of the buttons from his coat. He handed it to her. 'Show this to the First Cantor.'

'And tell her what?' Janva asked.

Kest turned and set off down the road, pausing only long enough to say, 'Tell her you're one of us.'

THE END

DUEL WITH THE DEMON

A TALE OF THE GREATCOATS

SEBASTIEN de CASTELL

THERE'S MORE THAN ONE KIND OF DEMON ...

King's Magistrate Estevar Borros prefers investigating supernatural crimes to overseeing mundane trials, but when an inexplicable fight breaks out in his courtroom, he's forced to duel a spirit viler than he's ever known.

1

PLEADINGS

Sparks erupted where the steel blades met, floating down to the loose hay covering the hall's stone floor. Were it not for the storm raging outside and the raindrops leaking through the rotted rafters of the roof, the old castle might've been set ablaze by the reckless fury of the two brothers.

At least, Estevar assumed they were brothers. Surely two such identically brutish and irredeemably stupid men could not have come from different fathers.

The nearly hundred and twenty townsfolk in attendance had seemed troubled when first the fight had broken out, but now several among them were cheering and whooping the assailants on, slapping the backs of the heads of those who failed to join in.

'Gentlemen, you will desist,' Estevar called out impatiently.

The criminally uncomfortable oak and iron Magistrate's chair in which he'd spent the better part of the day wedged like a hog caught in the fork of a tree root wore on his temper. The stench of too many bodies pressed too close together, of ale and pipeweed snuck inside the improvised courtroom, all of it had been making Estevar's head swim for hours.

And now this.

'Who are those two hooligans?' Estevar asked the girl who'd been serving as his clerk today.

'Rugio and Raballo, my Lord,' she replied, half-hidden behind his chair.

'And what is your name?'

The black-haired waif in the dull and faded grey-green dress stuck her head out from behind the chair. All-day she'd struck him as clever and confident, yet now she was positively terrified by this petty brawl. 'My name is Abria, my Lord.'

Estevar tugged at the lapels of his dark leather great-coat to straighten it, as well as to make sure some of the smaller weapons secreted within were in easy reach. If the girl was this frightened over what appeared to be little more than two men having it out with one another, perhaps she knew something he did not.

'Well, Abria, I am a Magistrate, not a nobleman, and so you may refer to me as "Your Eminence" – though I warn you,' he said with a wink to keep from frightening her further, 'I'll know if you're commenting on my physique. Alternately you may simply call me Estevar.'

'Yes, Your Emin—' the girl paused, openly contemplating his girth. 'Yes, Estevar.'

Wise child.

'Now,' Estevar went on, 'would you kindly explain to

me why, given the Town Masters of Sen Trovan requested one of the King's Travelling Magistrates come all this way to judge cases long overdue, the constables are tolerating an unsanctioned duel in this . . .' he glanced around at the ruinous condition of the town's uninhabited castle, '. . . delightful cathedral to civility and good government?'

Abria pointed to the two men who continued to swing their longswords at each other wildly as chips of stone and mortar flew from this ancient castle's walls, coming apart under the onslaught of time, disrepair, and the steel blades of two men who clearly knew nothing about the weapons they wielded so recklessly. 'Rugio and Raballo are the constables.'

Saint Ethalia-who-shares-all-sorrows, Estevar swore silently.

How had it all gone so badly? Thirty-one cases had been put before him during the nine hours since he'd arrived in Sen Trovan this morning, soaked through despite his leather greatcoat and dragging an equally wet and irritable mule behind him, all so he could hear cases held for nearly six months as those with grievances awaited a Magistrate. So many injustices, great and small; so much misery suffered by those unable to buy or fight their way out of trouble.

Now Estevar was going to have to part two overgrown boys with the flat of his own rapier – assuming he could free himself from the chair and not wind up waddling towards the belligerents with it still attached to his buttocks.

A throne, the town masters had dubbed this cruelly stiff torture device. The original seat of governance of the

Margrave who once ruled this march, they'd assured him. Now the tiny castle with its lone hall and wrecked outbuildings served as a tavern, an occasional barn, and, for today at least, a courtroom.

Estevar's courtroom.

He squeezed himself out from between the throne's torturously curved iron arms that had been pressing against his bladder all afternoon and reached for the scabbarded rapier resting against a broken stone column that had once supported the roof and now served only as a reminder that this was probably a bad place to be when it finally collapsed.

Why couldn't the new First Cantor of the Greatcoats have continued Estevar's unique status within the King's Travelling Magistrates? Most of them despised dealing with matters of the supernatural. They preferred simple, sensible legal quandaries and the occasional duel to enforce their verdicts so they could show off how daring and vigorous they were. Estevar enjoyed a fine meal, a good glass of wine, and the intellectual challenge of solving a murder for which the only suspect was a ghost or demon or some bedevilled frog.

Give me a good curse or case of possession over this devilry any day, he thought.

'There are too few of us left,' Chalmers had informed him with the world-weary wisdom of an eighteen-year-old newly elevated to First Cantor describing the state of the country to a man twice her age who'd been judging cases since before she'd shed her baby teeth. 'People have gotten so used to lawlessness they don't know anything else anymore. They need to see the Greatcoats, Estevar, and believe again that every crime, every injustice, will be met with the full force of the King's Travelling Magistrates.'

One of the supposed constables went flying over an already battered wooden table at the other end of the hall. That the two had shed their longswords and begun wrestling like quarrelsome pigs in a sty was a further indication of both their drunkenness and their rank stupidity.

How had this senseless brawl started, anyway? Estevar had nearly come to the end of the case list. His only ambition for his first day had been to hear the plaintiff's declarations and, where a defendant bothered to answer, their defences or counter-claims. With the necessary collection of testimony, gathering of evidence, litigation, and rendering of verdicts – to say nothing of any duels Estevar might have to fight should the losing side demand trial by combat – he would already have been trapped in this leaking, stinking ruin for weeks.

Now he'd be lucky if half those seeking legal remedies or reprieves didn't abandon their suits entirely, fearing no mere Magistrate could offer them lasting justice.

Perhaps this precocious First Cantor is right, he thought, striding through the crowd towards the combatants. *The citizens of Tristia have been deprived the benefit of the King's Laws for so long, they no longer trust in either their protections or the consequences of breaking them.*

The fracas was growing as two other assailants – a man and a woman who Estevar had assumed were lovers given their hands had been so frequently buried beneath each other's clothing during the hearings – had joined in the fray as well. On opposite sides.

That woman . . . hadn't he seen her whispering to one of the brothers before the fight started? And now others were being drawn into the brawl, too, as any semblance of civility was being battered out of these people.

No more.

The longer Estevar bore witness to these events, the more convinced he became that his youthful superior had been correct: It had been too long since folk had reckoned with a true duelling Magistrate.

He took a deep breath into his voluminous lungs, ignored the tickle in his throat that likely signalled that a day spent being dripped on from a leaky roof had left him with the beginnings of a cold, and drew his rapier from its sheath.

'Good people of Sen Trovan!' he bellowed. His voice rattled the rafters above and threatened to bring down the roof on all of them. 'This bedlam is beneath your dignity and robs those who came here to have their cases heard of a chance at justice. Such wanton barbarism enslaves you. Allow me to free you from the chains of ill-temper and chicanery.'

The combatants stopped and turned, along with those of their fellow residents trying to flee the mayhem. Sen Trovan had rid itself of its corrupt Margrave years ago and was now led by a committee of merchants and artisans known as the Twelve Masters. These men and women were granted authority by vote of their fellow citizens in exchange for promises of prosperity and good order, neither of which, so far as Estevar could tell, they had delivered.

Prosperity is beyond my abilities to promise, my friends,

Estevar thought as he made his way across the hay and horseshit-covered floor towards the ever-growing warring factions. *Order, however, it shall be my pleasure to provide.*

At first, they all stood staring at him, this big-bellied southerner with his swarthy complexion, his oiled black hair and carefully-trimmed beard that ended in beaded braids just below the collar of his long leather greatcoat. What a buffoon he must have seemed to them. A foreigner, in appearance, if not in fact.

Good, he thought. *Let the lesson be all the sharper.*

They waited for him to explain himself, but he remained silent. When one attempted to tamp down the flames of violence, those who wished it to continue would inevitably make themselves heard.

'Who do you think you are?' demanded the woman who was still holding the shattered clay mug she'd used to knock the man Estevar had assumed was her lover senseless. She was bigger than she'd first seemed, perhaps forty years old but fighting-fit, with strong shoulders bared by a sleeveless shirt over loose-fitting cotton trousers. The belt she wore had twin dagger sheathes near the back – perfect for an unexpected draw. Along the muscles of her right forearm were roughly-inked tattoos of skulls. Eight of them. Estevar was not familiar with this particular form of self-ornamentation, but the symbolism was easy enough to discern – and was made patently clear when she picked up a discarded longsword and brought it into guard.

So it's you who set this all in motion, he thought. *Just when I was about to hear the last cases and schedule the trials, you set one of the brothers against the other.*

'My Lord, don't!' Abria whispered furiously, standing close behind Estevar. 'You don't want to pick a fight with her. She practically rules Sen Trovan!'

'What did I tell you about calling me, "Lord"?' he asked quietly as he gently pushed her out of the way of their sword blades. 'And besides, it seems to me this fight was picked before I even arrived in your lovely town.'

Truth be told, Estevar's strict and rather old-fashioned upbringing had imbued him with a disinclination to fight women, but the many fencing bouts he'd lost to the nearly half of the Greatcoats who were female had cured him of that reticence.

He gave the instigator a curt bow followed by the sweeping salute of his rapier.

'My Lady, perhaps you failed to hear when I introduced myself earlier today. I am Estevar Valejan Duerisi Borros, a Greatcoat of the King's Travelling Magistrates. Should either my name or my rank be too complicated for you to remember, I will happily etch them both upon your backside with the tip of my blade unless you desist immediately.'

Before she could formulate a response, he turned to the other combatants. 'The rest of you, form a line.'

'A line?' asked a middle-aged man in blacksmith's apron bearing a mallet he'd had no business bringing to a courtroom. 'What for?'

Estevar smiled amiably. 'So that anyone else who chooses to disrupt these proceedings may await their turn. Many of your brethren came here today with petitions for justice that have gone unheard not merely for months, but in some cases years, and by every Saint and Devil, I will hear those cases, and I shall render my verdicts. If some of you prefer the ways of lawlessness, of the strong taking from the weak, then get in line, damn you, for if it's violence you crave, then there is only one question you need answer me.'

Estevar Borros turned his attention back to the woman with the longsword and the eight tattooed skulls across her forearm. He spread his own arms wide, making a target of his belly, and asked, 'Shall we begin?'

2

ALLEGATIONS

In a perfect world, the combination of Estevar's appeal to decency and the threat of duelling one of the King's legendary Greatcoats would've induced the fine citizens of Sen Trovan to abandon their ill tempers and disrespect for the suffering of their neighbours in favour of the peaceful settlement of disputes. But this was Tristia, where equal justice forever struggled to find a foothold, and a Magistrate – especially one who looked like Estevar – represented the very epitome of all they resented about the outside world.

The tattooed woman – Celize she was called, judging by the hoots and howls from her followers among the crowd as she stalked Estevar with her borrowed longsword – was a canny street fighter. She'd wisely removed her shoes, her bare feet affording her surer purchase on the damp straw all over the floor. She crouched low, making herself a smaller target while loading her powerful thighs so she could spring at Estevar when the time was right. All the while she hurled insults at him, mocking his almost dance-like fencer's steps almost as much as his appearance.

'We don't take to noblemen around here, Trattari,' she said, emphasizing the customary slur used to belittle Greatcoats. 'When the old Margrave died, we chased away his worthless offspring.' She swung the blade of her longsword in a double arc, first knocking the point of Estevar's rapier aside and then going for a slash at his knees. As he drew back just enough to evade the cut, she whispered, 'I put his two littlest boys to the sword myself.'

Estevar brought his point back into line, using his back foot to shove away a broken piece of stone from the floor that threatened to slip beneath his boot heel.

'I don't care much for noblemen myself, madam,' he said. 'Nor do I have an opinion on how a people choose to govern themselves. I do confess to a strong dispassion for murderers and those who seek to incite riots. I thank you for bringing another case to my docket that I may pursue in earnest once our duel has ended, assuming both of us are still alive.'

He still hadn't made a move against her, partly because he wanted to gauge her style before he committed himself to a lunge, and partly because there was so much about this strange situation he didn't yet understand.

Celize took his hesitation for weakness and managed to spit in his face despite the seven feet distance between them. A prodigious accomplishment, he thought.

'Ponce!' she shouted, then tried getting the crowd to join in. 'Ponce! Ponce! Ponce!'

She is clever, Estevar observed, watching the way she moved. *With her tongue she makes it seem as if she underestimates me, yet she knows the range of my rapier's thrust exceeds the cut of her longsword. She derides my style as if to suggest there's no danger to her or anyone who gets in my way during the fight.*

That, he realized abruptly, was her strategy. Celize would seek to rile up the bystanders, get them into the kind of boisterous pushing and shoving that goes with a tavern brawl. Estevar would thus become ever more boxed in by the crowd, which would in turn remove the advantage of his longer blade and superior skill.

Perhaps this is the real reason why Chalmers insisted you ride this backwoods circuit, he told himself as he evaded a pair of wild slashes from Celize aimed at making him stumble on the uneven floor of the great hall. *You enjoy the bizarre supernatural cases because they appeal to your curiosity and sense of wonder, but while you've been off chasing tales of ghosts, the country has itself become possessed by an altogether mundane form of evil.*

'Look at him run!' Celize guffawed, brazenly ignoring the possibility he might be drawing her in. 'Come on, boys! Let's give his Eminence's bottom a shove, eh?'

Several men and women slipped around the battered old furniture to work their way behind Estevar. Others began shoving tables to pen him in tighter. All too soon Estevar saw he'd underestimated how easily a mob was forming under Celize's expert direction.

To interfere in a lawful duel! he thought despairingly. The one tradition respected by the Tristian people since the days when trial by combat had been the means by which they'd wrested their freedom from those who'd brought them to this island to languish and die in the mines beneath the ground.

Many nations had some form of trial by combat, but in Tristia it was elevated to a complex system of duella civitas and interagito, verdeto, condamno and so many more. It seemed a point of pride among Tristians that duelling in this country was as close to fair as violence could be.

Yet here, now, a Magistrate might well find himself held down by a maddened crowd so that a woman who had likely bullied and belittled half of them could tear him apart at her leisure.

The first push from behind nearly sent Estevar into his opponent's outstretched blade. He managed to knock it away with his rapier, but the price was a sharp ache in his ankle where a broken stone tile slipped out beneath his right foot.

Celize gave him a murderer's grin, full of teeth and malice and good cheer.

'Look at him,' she called out to the others. 'Comes here, to our town, sets himself down in his little throne, and tells us he's going to decide what's right and what's wrong. Does that sound right to any of you?'

Several of her confederates roared their outrage, and Estevar noted many who had come here pleading with him to hear their cases were cowed by the glares of Celize and her allies. What a fool he'd been! The scheme was so simple it barely deserved the name, and yet it had worked brilliantly.

The list of cases to be brought before a Magistrate is kept strictly secret. The Town Masters had assured him this was the case here. So Celize had allowed those cases to be presented publicly today so that she could identify who had filed suits, which, though not directly linked to her, nonetheless interfered with her interests in Sen Trovan. Perhaps the final plaintiffs on the list had even intended to name her explicitly. Before that could happen, she had started the fight, fanned the flames until it grew into a brawl so that she could halt the hearings before Estevar could set the trials, and tonight she and her cohort would've paid visits to those with cases she didn't want pursued.

No wonder the Town Masters had failed to deliver the peace and tranquility for which their constituents longed. No wonder this castle was being allowed to languish, never turned into a proper town hall or to some other communal use. This Celize had likely been using her influence to ensure a constant, simmering chaos beneath which she could gradually build control.

'We chased away his worthless offspring,' she had said of the dead Magrave. 'I put his two little boys to the sword myself.'

A tall, long-limbed man on his right flank tried to sneak up and grab his arm, but Estevar was keeping track of everyone's position in the hall now. With a casual, almost accidental-seeming flick of his slender rapier blade, he sent the fellow scurrying away with a bleeding gouge across his palm.

'Fast ain't you, for such a big boy,' Celize said quietly enough that only he could hear over the cheers and jeers of the crowd. 'But things are just starting to heat up. Can you feel it, Magistrate? The way the sweat starts to smell different when the blood boils?'

One of her allies took advantage of the confusion to shove a young woman who couldn't have been more than fifteen right into the path of Estevar's rapier. He had to pull his weapon up high, reach out a hand and grab hold of the terrified girl's arm, steady her and push her behind him so she could get away before having to take Celize's slashing blow with the heavier longsword against his sharper but weaker blade. She was strong, this one, and for a moment he feared the blade would shatter, but it held; the Greatcoats don't ride out on their judicial circuits with their second-best swords.

'Not bad,' Celize conceded, circling him as she both vied for position against him and gave her associates the means to evade his sight. 'How long do you think you can keep it up? Face it, Magistrate, you don't belong here. You don't know what a good old-fashioned night of knives looks like in Sen Trovan. You came all this way thinking to show us how the world works, but you don't understand our world at all.'

Estevar wiped the sweat from his forehead. Everything about this situation worked against him. The unfamiliar terrain, the unbearable heat from the crowds, and the way Celize so willingly turned chaos to her advantage.

'You're wrong, my Lady,' he said then, for despite all that had occurred, he was still Estevar Borros, the King's Crucible, and sword fighting was not his only talent. 'Among the Greatcoats, I am known for separating ghosts from ghost stories, from recognizing the difference between trickery and demonic possession.'

Celize laughed, attempting a slash at his legs even as someone in the crowd threw a clay mug at his head. He dropped low, raised his forearm to take the blow on the curved bone plate in the sleeve of his greatcoat. His arm went numb, but the plate held.

'Is that what I am then?' Celize asked, skipping back before he could deliver his own thrust. 'A demon?'

Estevar rose to spin on his back heel, delivering a slash from the tip of his rapier against the cheeks of first one and then a second of Celize's accomplices, only to resume his en guarde posture and wink at Celize herself.

'There are, it turns out, rather few demons afoot in Tristia,' he told her. 'A depressing revelation for a man whose chosen vocation is to seek out the supernatural. But you have done me a fine favour this day, my Lady, for I see now that even in the absence of demons and devils, still may diabolical possession plague a town such as this one. You thought to prevent the airing of your insidious influence over your fellow citizens by engaging me in this duel, but there you have made a mistake, for I am, as you have called me, a Magistrate, and I am more than happy to elicit testimony at the point of a blade.'

Even as she leaped up high to attempt a devastating downward cut against him, Estevar said, 'Let the exorcism begin.'

3

TESTIMONY

'How many of you came before me today testifying to barns or workshops set on fire?' Estevar asked, holding Celize at bay with a mix of feints followed by lightning-fast thrusts for which she could not tell the difference and had to fall back. When one of her allies in the crowd tried to interfere, he stabbed his blade in their direction like an accusing finger. 'Perhaps you saw this fellow here nearby the night of the crime?' he asked.

The crowd turned to gape at the wiry man trying to hide a club by his right leg. The man slunk back.

'Or was it her?' Estevar asked then, taking from the pocket of his greatcoat a tiny spiked ball barely larger than his thumb and hurling it into the palm of a woman about to shove another unwitting victim into the fray.

Celize's confederate screeched in pain.

'I saw her!' a boy said. 'She was carrying a torch the night my aunt's tannery went up in flames.'

'You saw nothing, boy,' Celize called out to him. 'If you know what's good for you.'

'Alas,' Estevar said. 'An accusation has been levelled. Tomorrow I will make further inquiries. You'd be surprised how willing people are to come forward once a suspect has been identified.'

Estevar wasn't one for lunges – his bulk made them somewhat risky affairs if he needed to recover quickly – but he allowed himself one now. Celize saw it coming, of course, and sidestepped to her right, but she had never been the target.

'Saints!' screamed a stoop-backed man who'd been about to hand Celize a small cloth pouch. The sack fell to the ground, tiny glittering grains pouring out of it as the fellow's hands went to the new wound on his leg.

'Throwing powdered glass into an opponent's face in the middle of a duel?' Estevar tut-tutted at Celize. 'Poor form, my Lady. Poor form. And one wonders whether your assistant in this rather pathetic magic trick hasn't a history of acting on your behalf?'

'He does,' said a heavyset woman with the tanned features of a farmer. 'That's the man I saw poisoning my crops last season, as I was going to present in my case tomorrow. The Town Masters said there wasn't no reason to explain why he'd do such a thing, but now it's clear it's because Celize wanted me to sell a portion of our land and I refused.'

'How curious,' Estevar said, breathing hard yet undeterred from pursuing this course of action. 'It almost seems as if anyone who intervenes for her has been suspected of some crime or other here in Sen Trovan.'

Celize became agitated then, realizing that soon none of her allies would risk aiding her for fear of being identified for some other offence committed on her behalf.

'Damn you and your Trattari tricks, you bastard foreigner!' she shouted as she swung wildly at him with her longsword.

'No,' he said calmly, allowing his greater stride and growing familiarity with the uneven flooring to pull her farther and farther off balance. 'Damn you, Celize of Sen Trovan. Damn you for teaching me that there are viler spirits at work in this country than the ones I've so long pursued!'

Estevar's elaborate, almost playful fencing style enraged her, but it was his words that stole her composure. With a vicious, almost mindless leap high in the air, she dropped the point of her longsword down at a diagonal angle to drive it into the gap between his collar and his neck, and from there hilt-deep into his body.

Estevar had always been a big man and had learned early on in his fencing training that speed of body would never be attainable to him. So he'd learned subtlety and precision: subtlety of mind, and precision of movement. Instead of retreating, he shuffled towards Celize six inches – just enough for her blade to go past his shoulder and slide down the back of his coat without piercing it. With his left hand, Estevar reached around her waist, and for a moment it was almost as if the two of them were dancing together.

As she drew away from him in disgust, he let his left hand slide along her right arm, and by the time she pulled away, her longsword was now in his hand.

'You have had your say, Celize of Sen Trovar,' he said to her as he spun the point of the blade around and rested it against her neck. 'Are you prepared now to hear my verdict?'

All went silent then. The crowd had pressed back away from the combatants. Those among them who might have aided Celize before were now too afraid of being identified as her confederates – especially given that others among the citizens of Sen Trovan were beginning to think there could indeed be a chance for proper trials to be held in their beleaguered town, even if the price was that they might have to partake of the risk required. In that stillness, everyone waited to see the killing thrust that would end Celize's life.

'Go on then,' she dared Estevar, though she did a poor job of hiding her fear. 'Get it over with.'

Estevar shook his head. 'Alas, my Lady, I have too long studied the supernatural to risk a foul-tempered spirit such as yours haunting me from beyond the grave. Besides, as you keep reminding me, I'm a Magistrate.'

With a jerk of his arm, he sent her longsword spinning up in the air, almost to the rafters. As it came back to earth, he caught it by the blade and brought the pommel crashing down on Celize's skull. Her eyes blinked several times before she fell to the hay-covered floor.

'We never sentence a suspect without first giving them a proper trial.'

4

CLOSING ARGUMENTS

Estevar was exhausted by the time he returned to the castle's hall the next morning. He'd almost considered cancelling the day's hearings, being covered in bruises and aches from his duel. But it seemed to him the people of Sen Trovan had already waited far too long to receive a fair hearing from a Magistrate, and so, after an hour of seeing to his still-irritated mule's needs, he hauled himself up the hill from the inn where he'd stayed the night to begin the day's proceedings.

'Saint Marta who-shakes-the-lion,' he swore when he entered the castle ruins and saw what had been done there.

'We're early risers in these parts,' Abria said. The girl was wearing her same faded grey-green cotton dress as the day before, yet it seemed brighter on her somehow, and the girl herself stood taller.

There were dozens of people inside, all setting about

various tasks and repairs. The floors had been cleared of muck and scrubbed until the stone practically gleamed. There were still gaps in it, of course, but some of those had already been filled in with a few carefully chosen slabs of rock. Those furnishings not yet beyond repair had been cleaned and polished, and someone had even begun working on repairing the rotting rafters in the roof.

'We had a town meeting this morning,' Abria informed him in a tone that suggested as far as she was concerned she'd organized the whole thing herself. 'We elected new Town Masters.'

'And are you one of them?' Estevar asked. 'Shall I now address you as Damina Abria?'

She giggled. A lovely sound that echoed far more pleasantly in the hall this morning than he would've thought possible yesterday. 'No, I'm too young still. Next year, though, for sure. In the meantime, mine was the first proposal approved by the new assembly,' she said proudly, sweeping an arm wide at the great stone hall. 'We'll be re-consecrating this as the official town hall. A place we can all come together when problems need solving.' She poked his belly through his leather greatcoat – a hanging offence so far as Estevar Borros was concerned, yet he found himself giggling as well. 'You know, so we don't have to wait on pretentious Greatcoats to come riding through town and looking down their noses at us.'

She meant it in jest, Estevar knew, yet there was some truth to her words. 'My dear, if I have given such an impression . . .' he paused. 'Which I fear I have indeed, I will begin the day with an apology to your fellow townsfolk.'

'Thank the Gods. That'll solve all our problems,' the girl said, rolling her eyes. 'In the meantime, we decided there's a more practical favour you can do for us.'

'If it's within my means,' he said.

Abria – who Estevar was now quite sure would be running this town when next his judicial circuits brought him back here – nodded to two burly young men at the back of the hall who went into the anteroom behind a newly-placed woven curtain. 'It's rather hard for people to pay attention to the rulings of a Magistrate who looks like he's two seconds from bursting out of his chair. Fortunately, my uncle and his man are the best carpenters in town.'

The two men returned from the anteroom bearing the old throne that had plagued Estevar yesterday, but now the seat had been widened by taking it apart and inserting a new piece in the middle, and the iron arms had been reshaped to accommodate a fuller physique. Someone had even had the kindness to fashion a cushion of the perfect shape and size, and already his buttocks were feeling relieved.

The men and women stopped in their labours to watch as Estevar made his way to the new Magistrate's throne of Sen Trovan. They clapped and cheered as he took his seat.

Estevar had been a Greatcoat for over fifteen years, had dined with Dukes, slept in palaces, and witnessed more wonders of the supernatural than perhaps any other person alive. Yet as he sat down in that chair and saw the fierce pride in Abria's eyes, and then in those of all in attendance who'd taken the first steps to take back the

242 | SEBASTIEN DE CASTELL

destiny of their town, it seemed to him that he had only just begun to discover the miracles that filled this strange country he called home.

THE END

WHEN THE SWORD SEEMS TO SMILE

A TALE OF THE GREATCOATS

SEBASTIEN de CASTELL

THE PRICE OF VICTORY

Falcio val Mond and the Greatcoats have brought Tristia
back from the brink of war and ruin, prevented the rise of
a dictator, and finally seen the King's heir returned to the
throne. What follows proves to be much, much harder for
Falcio...

1

WHEN THE SWORD SEEMS TO SMILE

It's a strange thing to watch the rise and fall of your wife's belly as she sits by the fire. With each sleepy breath – hers, not mine – the gentle slope beneath the pale blue cotton shift swells as if any moment now the baby's going to leap out of her, expecting me to catch it.

And what am I supposed to do after that?

Ethalia exhales, and the moment where I unbuckle my duelling swords forever, shed the long leather coat that has marked me as one of the King's Travelling Magistrates these past fifteen years to take on the newer and far more terrifying mantle of fatherhood recedes a little while longer.

I can't decide whether my own breathing comes easier when Ethalia is inhaling or exhaling. I know she's aware of me, of both my anticipation and my doubts. She's always known what I was feeling, even before she became a Saint.

A real one. I'm not being metaphorical here: my wife is

now known in this troubled little country of ours as Saint Ethalia who-shares-all-sorrows. I'm most commonly referred to as 'That arsehole Falcio val What's-his-name'.

Father.

Soon someone will be calling me father, and that will change everything. It will change *me*.

It has to, doesn't it?

I lean back in my chair, closer to the wooden-slatted window of this tiny cottage we've rented until the baby is born and we're able to make our way by boat to a little island off the coast of Baern that is Ethalia's birthright. She tells me it's beautiful. Peaceful. The folk who live there work out their differences with words over rabbit stew instead of steel inside a duelling circle.

Who knew such strange cultural practices still existed in which violence wasn't the inevitable answer to every question?

I'm calmer now, and for a moment I tell myself it's alright; I'm growing accustomed to this impending and uncertain future. But then I notice the reason for my composure: the fingers of my right hand have slipped around the leather grip of the scabbarded rapier that sits across my lap at night when Ethalia dozes and I listen by the window in case any of the thousand enemies this same blade has earned me should come to call. The reassurance I've learned to feel when holding a blade is an instinct that's kept me alive all these years when by rights I should've been dead a hundred times over.

Outside the wind is swirling the fallen Autumn leaves. Weasels and field mice and the damned cat who sings louder than a Bardatti Troubadour half the night are all scampering about in search of dinner. Owls and night larks patrol the forest canopy, hoping to snatch up a tasty mouse or weasel or perhaps even the cat. When those efforts fail, I hear the scrape of their claws settling on the tree branches, followed by frustrated hoots or caws or whatever the hells those assorted screeches are called.

It's a veritable cacophony out there. And yet, amidst all that noise, still I could make out the faintest footstep of a Dashini assassin should one dare to approach this cottage – should one even think about coming near my wife and unborn child.

'Come on, you bastards,' I mutter quietly to myself. 'I dare you.'

'You're doing it again.'

I practically leap out of my chair. Yesterday when she surprised me like that I lurched out of it so forcefully I broke the damned thing and had to spend most of today repairing it – poorly. Somewhere in the last fifteen years of riding across the country, hearing cases, rendering verdicts, fighting duels to enforce those verdicts, going on nigh-impossible missions, and once facing off against a God – an actual *God* - I seem to have forgotten to learn carpentry.

'Doing what, dear?' I ask.

Ethalia smiles at me in that way that says I won't succeed in fooling her - now or ever. She tilts her head a fraction as she leans back against her own chair, sending the dark curls of her hair tumbling across her left shoulder. I badly want to go over there and smooth one particularly unruly wisp, perhaps let my fingers linger a moment or two against her skin. A kiss wouldn't be untoward, surely? Perhaps even—

'I'm not a porcelain doll, Falcio,' she says, watching me. 'There's nothing to stop us making love except your absurd terror of squishing a baby who, at this moment, is roughly the size of an acorn.'

'A squish-able acorn,' I insist.

She rolls her eyes. 'Must I come over there and seduce you?'

Now *that* sounds like an excellent idea.

'I could dance naked for you,' I suggest and raise my hips off the chair to wiggle them. 'While I've never performed on a stage, I've always assumed I'd be terribly good at it.'

At last, I win a genuine laugh from her, and it's as if the entire cottage had been constructed by master architects just to project that laugh to my ears.

An instant later, I'm on my feet, hurtling outside the cottage with my rapier drawn from its scabbard and a devil drumming inside my chest.

'I heard you, you son of a bitch! Show yourself so I can teach you the first rule of the sword!'

There's no reply but the sounds of footsteps running off into the forest.

Fast, I think. *Sure-footed. He knows the terrain better than me, but I've got the longer stride.*

I'm about to race off in pursuit when I feel Ethalia's hand on my arm. 'A footpad,' she informs me. 'Nothing more. The crofter told us they roam the woods at night searching for unattended cottages. They're no threat to us.'

'Damned right,' I mutter, holding up my rapier. The blade gleams in the moonlight with a kind of promise.

Ethalia gives a polite cough.

'Hmm?' I ask.

She tugs on my arm, turning me towards her, and I see now the glimmering of my blade was caused not by the moon or stars above but by the fact that my wife glows sometimes. Literally glows. I'm still not being metaphorical.

'You seem to forget, my darling,' she tells me in that soft, gentle way that suggests she's not nearly so soft and gentle as I might sometimes prefer, 'that one of us is a Saint and has rather a good deal more power with which to reprimand would-be pilferers than a sharpened stick.'

'It's a rapier, Ethalia. One of the finest in all of Tris—'

'Yes, dear, it's a lovely sharpened stick.' She slips her arm in mine and leads me to the path that meanders through the forest. 'Let's walk off some of this tension of yours and you can tell me all about how your pointy stick is the finest in the land.'

We've walked this path a hundred times by now and I know every upturned rock and low-hanging tree branch. I've noted every spot from which an ambush could be launched and considered all the ways the terrain could be turned to my advantage.

There is, unquestionably, something very wrong with me. I try to push away the anticipation of unseen foes, focus my awareness instead on Ethalia's arm in mine, her head against my shoulder, and settle in for some gentle mockery and possibly well-deserved seduction.

'Tell me about it,' she says, bringing her lips close to my ear.

I reach a hand down the front of my trousers. 'Well, you know, it's a goodly size at the moment. I suppose it's all relative, and I haven't had occasion to measure it against that of other m—'

She bites my ear – not endearingly.

'Tell. Me. About. It.'

'I'm just . . .' How am I supposed to explain that violence isn't something you can take off and put on like a sword belt. It's either in you day and night or it fades, and when it fades, you're no longer the duellist you once were. You've lost the ability to protect the people you love from the ones who despise you.

And in case I forgot to mention it, I have a *lot* of enemies.

Ethalia puts a finger to my lips, halting our progress along the path. 'If you start up on the sad tale of poor Falcio val Mond and his endless guilt over those he thinks he's failed and how he can't possibly imagine ever failing his new wife and unborn child and oh, woe is our Falcio for his sense of duty demands he remain a paragon of valour, I'm going to set my Saint's Awe upon you and have you genuflect at my feet until morning.'

'Well, normally I'd remind you that Greatcoats kneel to no one, not even Kings, but in this case . . .'

I drop to my knees. The forest floor is cool, and I can feel the faint dampness through the fabric of my trousers. The ground is neither too dry nor too wet, and will provide an excellent grip should someone—

I'm doing it again.

'You don't need to unleash your Awe upon me to get me to do a little groveling,' I tell her. 'All you have to do is ask.'

'Excellent,' she says, pulling me back up to my feet. 'Now tell me about it.' She takes my hand and reaches across my waist to place it on the pommel of my rapier, which I've been working very hard these past few minutes to leave in its scabbard. 'Not your fears, Falcio, not your guilt.'

'What then?'

She tugs on my arm and we resume our walk. There's a bend in the path up ahead. I keep one eye on it as Ethalia explains what she needs from me.

'There's a moment,' she begins, her fingertips tapping on the back of my hand, 'when your fingers first wrap themselves around the hilt of a sword, before the grimace that comes to your lips, before the oaths or threats or clever retorts. It's like . . .' she hesitates as if lost for words. Ethalia is *never* lost for words. One side of her mouth rises just a fraction, and in the dim light of the stars above I can just make out those crinkles at the corners of her eyes that I adore. 'It's like a smile,' she continues, pressing my hand more firmly to the rapier's leather grip. 'Not of anticipation for the fight or bloodlust or anything like that. It's as if, for just one instant, you're . . . you're leaping off the edge of a cliff, no idea if the water's deep enough below or you'll crash on the rocks. Not fearless, but . . .' she shakes her head. 'I can't put my finger on it. I swear it's been driving me mad since the day I met you.' Those ocean-blue eyes of hers rise to meet mine. 'So tell me about it.'

'I can't. I don't . . . Ethalia, I don't know what you're

talking about.' I tug the rapier from the scabbard, revealing an inch of the blade. 'Most of the time when this thing's in my hand, I'm beyond terrified. I'm lucky because most fencers lose themselves to raw instinct and conditioning during a fight, but my brain slows. I start seeing the duel as a puzzle. A machine whose gears I just need to figure out to make it work in my favour. I think that's why I've survived this long. But it's not anything like you're describing.'

'Perhaps the moment's too fleeting and in all that puzzle-solving you're doing, you forget what you felt.'

'It's possible, I suppose.'

Ethalia chews on her lower lip a moment. I haven't seen her do that before. She's quiet, and the silence between us is filled by the breeze that sends the leaves swirling about our feet. Oh, and that stupid cat's started up again.

'Close your eyes,' she says abruptly.

'Why?'

'An experiment.'

'What?'

'You heard me. Close your eyes. I want to try something.'

I have come to learn, in recent years, that I am absolutely rubbish with women. However, I've also discovered that if you simply do exactly what they tell you, you'll only get the signal wrong about fifty percent of the time, which is, oddly, a vastly superior result to the one that comes from me second-guessing them.

'Fine,' I say, first moving us beneath the bough of a

thick-trunked tree that will protect our backs should anyone . . .

'My eyes are closed,' I tell her. 'I am yours to command, Saint Ethalia who-shares-all-sorrows.'

'Excellent. Now, I want you to pretend you're out here on a terribly dangerous mission. One with Kest and Brasti at your side. Some horrible Viscount has committed an outrageous wrong against a local cowherd and you've ridden three hundred miles from Castle Aramor to take up his case and restore justice to our tangled nation – or at least, whichever patch of farmland this all happens on.'

With my eyes closed, I can't see her, but I can *hear* the smirk.

'You know, to a casual observer, it might sound as if you're mocking my righteous quest to save the world.'

'And cowherds,' she insists.

'Yes, including the cowherds.'

'Good. So, there the three of you are, about to do battle with a trio of armoured Knights wh—'

'A dozen.'

'What?' she asks.

'As long as we're manufacturing tales from whole cloth, let's make it memorable at least.'

'Fine. After a lengthy trial in which you've heard both sides of the case and rendered your verdict, the Viscount surprises you by calling forth a dozen of his most loyal Knights and commanding them to murder you.'

'And the cowherd,' I add. 'For some reason they always want to kill the cowherd, too.'

When next she speaks, Ethalia's voice is lower, breathier.

I can feel the warmth from her next to me, inhale the scent of her hair and taste the kiss she hasn't yet given me. It's hard to concentrate, but then she says the words, and like magic, I forget all about the forest and the rustling tree branches, the wind, and the owls and the damned cat yowling for its mate.

I'm standing on an open field. There's dung on my boots. The uncomfortable wooden kitchen chair someone brought out to serve as the magistrate's throne has fallen aside. I can feel the grassy turf bounce beneath my heels, just a fraction, as the twelve Knights in the grey and black colours of the Viscount of Sierac march towards us. The breeze picks up, and the stench of the oil they use to keep their steel breastplates and pauldrons shiny assails my nostrils.

'There's no way,' I mutter, noting the wide, grassy field without so much as a decent tree stump to use as an obstruction, no escape routes, no possibility of reaching our horses. Even if we could run, one of the Knights has already grabbed the cowherd who dared bring a case against the Viscount by the neck. There's a faint tearing sound as the wool of his only good shirt gives way under the iron grip of the Knight's gauntlet. 'There's no way we can do this,' I repeat.

In my mind's eye, I turn to Kest on my right. His face is as placid as those of the cows chewing the grass a few yards away. That's when I realize Kest is actually calculating whether our odds would improve if we somehow used those cows to our advantage.

'Six,' he says to me without my needing to ask.

'Only six?' Brasti says, an arrow already nocked to the string of his bow. It'll be Intemperance – the most

powerful of his three bows but also the heaviest and slow-
est. It's the only one with a chance to pierce those steel
breastplates. Otherwise he has to try for far narrower
targets, but the Knights have brought shields with them.

'You'll take three with the arrows,' Kest explains.
'Mostly because Falcio and I will be occupying almost all
of their attention. I'll kill two. Falcio will get one
before we—'

'Wait,' I say, putting a hand on his arm through the
sleeve of his greatcoat. Even as we prepare for this hope-
less fight, I can tell his muscles are relaxed. Supple. He's
long past worrying about death and dying. This is one of
the reasons Kest is the finest swordsman who ever lived.
'You're saying I only kill *one* of them before they overwhelm us?'

Kest shrugs, then nods to the scabbard at my side. 'I
keep telling you, rapiers are duelling weapons; they're ill-
suited to piercing armour.'

'I've killed plenty of Knights, I'll have you know. You
just have to get them in the soft spots. The opening on the
helmet or break the chain mail between their—'

'Is this part necessary?' Ethalia asks, momentarily
bringing me back to the forest and the breeze and the . . .
no, apparently the cat's managed to get himself laid now
and has called it a night.

'It's all part of it,' I insist, though I'm not really sure
what I'm talking about. 'This moment, right before the
weapons are drawn, when the enemy has you figured out
and they know – they *know* – this time they've got you.
When every tactic in every book on fencing and duelling
has been exhausted even before the first blow is struck,

when the Viscount or Margrave or hell, some petty criminal head of a gang is grinning from ear to ear because they're about to win, you're about to die, and the world will prove itself to be exactly the way they've always believed it was.'

'What happens next?' Ethalia asks me. 'If it's so impossible, why don't you give up? Beg for mercy? Try to negotiate some sort of deal?'

I feel a tightness at the corners of my mouth. Must just be the tension before the battle. Brasti is staring at me, that mixture of exasperation and tentative hope playing about those indecently handsome features of his.

'Ah,' he says.

'What?' Kest asks.

'Look. Falcio's making that face.'

'I don't make a face,' I say.

'You really do,' Ethalia tells me. 'Don't shy away from it, don't skip over it. Tell me what's happening right now.'

'I . . . I'm looking at the Knights. Not their weapons or their armour. I'm looking into their eyes, one at a time, and then the Viscount, and the cowherd, and all the people watching, not one of whom anyone believes will risk their own lives to save a trio of Greatcoats nobody wanted coming here in the first place. I'm looking at the grass beneath my feet, and the dung – that beautiful, wondrous cow dung!'

'Cow dung?' someone asks, but now I'm not sure if it's Ethalia or Brasti.

I turn to Kest. 'Cow dung.'

Nobody knows what I'm talking about. I'm not even sure *I* know what I'm talking about, but Kest has been my friend since we were twelve years old, and Brasti has been a brother to us both since the King named him to the Greatcoats. That bond between us – that's part of the answer. 'It's the thing we have that the Knights don't,' I mutter.

'Friendship?' Ethalia asks.

I shake my head, and let my right hand dangle, my fingers tickled by the tall grasses growing in that imaginary field somewhere far away, smelling the oil from Kest's coat – he's always kept his better maintained than Brasti or I. The faint thrum as Brasti's bowstring as his fingertips play against it in anticipation of what's to come. It's not quite a melody, yet there's a song in it somewhere.

'The three of us believe in each other,' I tell Ethalia. 'Even more than we believe in ourselves. There's no fight we won't walk into together, no risk we won't share. It's not just because we're friends. It's because the three of us have seen the depth to which the world can sink into its own corruption and cynicism. We need to believe in something else. In something better. We have to make that belief true, prove that the impossible is . . .'

'Possible?' she asks.

I look back down at the cow dung and realize the source of my fascination is the way the twelve Knights surrounding us are so disgusted by it. They've served their master too well and been too richly rewarded for their efforts. When it comes at them, they'll flinch because they don't want any of it getting through their visors. When their armoured boots get too close to it, they'll try to shift away because of the embarrassment they'd feel in front of their fellows should they slip and fall in cow shit. From the hundred advantages they have over us, I find a thousand weaknesses that weren't there just moments before.

That's when my hand wraps around the hilt of my rapier, when I nod first to Kest, then to Brasti.

That's when the smile Ethalia's been asking me about comes to my face.

'No,' I tell her. 'We don't make the impossible possible.'

The sound of my rapier slipping from its scabbard is a shimmer in the air. It's the chime of a bell ringing in the only church I've ever found worthy of worship. It's defiance in the face of all the odds against us, and a sworn promise that a former peasant in a long leather coat with a sword he was never meant to wield is about to change not merely the world, but the rules by which the world works.

'We make the impossible inevitable,' I say aloud. 'Brasti calls it "swashbuckling". The term used to refer to something bravos once did when roaming the streets looking to pick a fight. They'd swash their rapiers against their buckler shields as a kind of taunt, daring better fencers to come challenge them. But that always struck me as petulant and self-serving. Brasti says he likes the word, though, and since we're the King's own Magistrates, he rendered his own verdict that from now on it meant—'

'Believing the impossible can be inevitable,' Ethalia finishes for me.

I nod, and in some part of my heart, Kest, Brasti and I are leaping into the fray against those damnable Knights, singing bawdy songs to offend their sensibilities and executing maneuvers so outrageous that only three people who love each other as we do would ever dare attempt them.

With a long, slow exhale, I say goodbye to the jumble of half-remembered memories and imaginings the two of us have conjured this night, and to the two men who will always remain my brothers regardless of when I put down the sword for good.

When I open my eyes, I see the tears in Ethalia's.

'What's wrong?' I ask, fearing this nostalgia she so badly wanted to explore has conjured a wall between us. But then she smiles, and I realize I've completely misread her.

'For weeks now,' she begins, taking my hand from the rapier and intertwining her fingers with mine, 'I've been trying to come up with a way to convince you that you'll be a good father, that you'll have something wonderful to give our daughter besides your fanatical need to protect her.' Ethalia's hand comes up to my cheek, her thumb tracing the line of my own smile that hasn't faded yet even though the memories have. 'This . . . this *swashbuckling*?'

I nod. It really is a strange word.

'*That* is the gift you'll give our child. That's the wonder you'll awaken inside her heart that will make all the other parts of you, Falcio, the good and the bad, make sense to her as she comes to know you and your history. It will be the bond between the two of you. Just the two of you, Falcio, and when she grows up . . . ' Ethalia lifts up the scabbard, and draws the rapier. It's not a perfect draw, of course, but I manage not to comment on it, and when the blade catches the light – both that of the crescent moon above and of my Sainted wife next to me – it gleams like a newborn star. Through all that shimmering, it's Ethalia's smile that shines brightest of all. 'Our daughter will know that a sword can be more than a weapon of violence. Maybe one day she'll even become ...'

The pause is there for me. You have to understand that Ethalia is properly named Ethalia who-shares-all-sorrows, the Saint of Mercy. Violence is anathema to her nature now. And yet, it's also a part of the life she's chosen with me, and she's been trying to find a way to let me see that I don't have to give up the man I am in order to be the one she and our daughter – and by the way, how in all the hells does she know we're having a daughter? Is that some new Saintly ability she hasn't apprised me of? Anyway, she's waiting for me to finish her sentence because that's the last step to getting me through the dark fog of fear and uncertainty that has been impenetrable for so long, that now parts before the blade the two of us hold together in our hands.

'A swashbuckler,' I say.

Ethalia's smile becomes a smirk, and as she kisses me at last, she says, 'I still think you should come up with a better name for it, but fine, my love. Our daughter will be a *swashbuckler*, in whatever way she chooses.'

I hold that kiss a long, long time, and for the first time in a long time, when I slide my rapier back in its scabbard, I'm content to leave it resting there, knowing it will always be a part of me, no longer ashamed of what it will mean to my daughter.

When at last our lips part, and Ethalia takes my hand to lead me back to our cottage, I find myself – despite the fact that I fully acknowledge I am rubbish with women and badly need to learn the skill of shutting my mouth when I'm ahead –saying something I never would've imagined until tonight.

'Damn, but I'm going to be an outstanding father.'

THE END

AFTERWORDS

NOTES ON THE STORIES

NOTES ON DEATH OF THE SWASHBUCKLER

My name is Falcio val Mond. I might just be the luck-iest man who ever lived.

Talk about asking for trouble. When Falcio uttered those last lines in Tyrant's Throne, the fourth and final volume of the Greatcoats Quartet, did he *really* believe it was going to be as easy as that?

Yes, and no.

He wasn't deceiving himself or the reader. He's not delusional (well, he's often delusional, but wasn't at that precise moment). But whether in love or friendship or – most pertinent of all – in duelling, Falcio has indeed been a very lucky man over the years. He's fought knights, brigands, half-mad indefatigable lunatics, entire mobs and, that one time, an actual god.

And he's lived to tell the tale.

But Falcio's no fool: he knows that one of these days, somebody's going to stick a blade in his heart.

In the pursuit of a set of ideals which few believe are attainable and many more resent as intrusions into their own rightful dominance, the First Cantor of the Great-coats has simply made too many enemies. Knights, Dukes, Dashini Assassins, Saints, and even the occasional God, Falcio has pissed off just about everyone at one point or another.

And he's tired.

Bruises, broken bones, stab wounds galore. He's been poisoned, cursed, and let's not forget the Greatcoat's Lament. All this done to a guy who's never even gotten over the trauma of losing his first wife.

Not to put too fine a point on it, but Falcio ain't Jack Reacher. He's survived on his wits, his daring, and the friendships that kept him sane and alive all these years. He may be a hero to some, but there's no "super" ahead of that word.

Few people know this, but in the very first draft of Traitor's Blade, Falcio died at the end. He got hit with the neatha poison and, surrounded by his closest friends and the daughter of his King, he passed peacefully into the afterworld. I knew this would never be the actual ending to the book, of course – that would be far too easy on Falcio. But I wanted to approach the story ready to see the end of its hero so that, for me, at least, every battle, every struggle, could prove to be his last.

So, too, with this tale.

Gavelle Sanprier, or an assassin like him, will one day come armed with just the right tools, just the right information, to catch Falcio unawares and do what so many others before failed to do.

And Falcio knows it.

So go ahead, all you would-be slayers of legends, all you ambitious murderers and conniving manipulators. Make your plans. Hatch your schemes. One of these days, whether because Falcio's lost his edge or simply because he's too tired to fight another duel, you're going to win.

But not today.

NOTES ON A STUDY IN STEEL

The rapier blades clink like wine glasses when the duel-lists cross swords for the first time.

Astute readers will have noticed the stylistic parallel between the opening of this tale and that of Duel With the Demon. I have a thing about opening stories with my figurative writer's camera close up on swordplay. It offers a means not only of visualizing the unfolding action but of showing the relationship between the action and the underlying themes of the story. In this case, that two weapons of violence should resemble the clinking of wine glasses is my way of showing the reader that there is something despicably refined – even fashionable – about the way blood is sometimes shed even in societies that consider themselves civilized. And shedding blood is so very fashionable in Rijou.

Little is written about the life of Aline, daughter of Paelis, prior to the events of Traitor's Blade. We know only that she was born to Lady Tiarren, a noblewoman of Rijou, and that her birth was the result of an adulterous affair with King Paelis. When we first meet Aline, she's covered in soot and coughing from the smoke created by the fire that slaughtered her mother's family and nearly took her with it. But who was she before that? What was her relationship like with the rest of the Tiarren family? Were they truly ignorant of her parentage, or were there suspicions raised in whispers that led to plots against her?

Telling her story too directly struck me as cliché: the young, clever chosen one who outwits her enemies. Instead, I wanted to explore someone else's plight – someone who might both bear witness to Aline's brilliant mind while also being unaware of her destiny. Percevar, raised in the intrigues and martial traditions of Rijou, yet too kind-hearted to follow in their footsteps, seemed an interesting foil to the world in which Aline is already becoming accustomed. The lessons he learns in this tale of swordplay and intrigue can never hope to shield her from the hordes of enemies coming for her, but they give her time – time to grow and refine her own techniques of survival. They also teach Percevar that if he ever hopes to put a stop to the endless games of violence that drive his society, he must first learn to win them.

NOTES ON DANCE OF THE CHAMBERLAIN

A corpse dangles from the chandelier in a Viscount's ballroom.

Dangles? No, *dances*.

That's all I started with. In fact, I began writing this story with nothing but the opening line you read on the first page. No clever scheme, no murderer, not even a main character. I like my mysteries to be, well, mysterious, and telling myself 'whodunnit' before I've started writing takes all the fun out of it.

The idea for Estevar Borros was born when it occurred to me that a Viscount would likely bring several advisors together to consult on what to do about a dead chamberlain's corpse dancing from a rope in his ballroom that no one could remove without suffering debilitating spiritual effects. Such advisors would, surely, have their own agendas, and likely bicker about the nature of these events.

So I wanted someone quiet. Someone contemplative who would wait until the others all had their say before informing them that they were entirely wrong. A man of stillness, like some of the old classic detectives. Poirot or Nero Wolf only with a sword and the occasional inclination to use it.

I had no idea who had killed the chamberlain nor what despicable necromancy had been perpetrated to leave him dancing from a rope two weeks after his death. So I did something unusual for me as a writer: I simply followed Estevar around in his mental and physical perambulations and waited for him to solve the crime for me.

Now, I'm not one of those writers who thinks his characters exist in their own right and whisper the next lines to be transcribed onto the page. I take responsibility for every word of fiction I write. However I do think one can, at times, with the right character, let the subconscious drive the process, moving ever forwards through the story with no assurances it will come to a meaningful and satisfying conclusion. I put my trust in Estevar's odd ways, his propensity to placidity when he can manage it, belligerence when his back is up, and above all, his approach that a Magistrate doesn't concern himself with the mystical or philosophical implications of events – only with the facts as they appear.

This dispassion towards the supernatural is what allows him to discern the need to recreate the music from the night of the murder to enable the chamberlain to stop dancing and find his voice. For Estevar, this is all a trial – one to which witnesses must be called, claims tested, and the guilty perpetrator sentenced. Magic and Gods be damned.

274 SEBASTIEN DE CASTELL

I'd never conceived of Estevar Valejan Duerisi Borros until the day he appeared on an otherwise blank page. Yet now I find myself wanting to write more of his stories, for though I've no idea how readers will receive him, I personally find the King's Crucible an interesting fellow to watch.

NOTES ON GRAVE OF THORNS

One of the consequences of recounting a fantasy epic through the eyes of a single character, as happens in the Greatcoats Quartet, is that hundreds of other stories are left untold. Falcio val Mond, the valorous and troubled narrator of that series witnessed many events unfold around him, but by necessity, was blind to countless others.

A hundred and forty-four Greatcoats were sent from Castle Aramor by King Paelis the night before he died, each one given a different mission, none of them knowing how theirs connected with those of their comrades. Some of those missions took the form of grand, heroic quests such as the King's command that Falcio "seek out my Charoites". Others came with broader purposes, such as Kest's burden to prevent Falcio from becoming a tyrant should the endless injustices of the world corrupt even him. Brasti's injunction to "keep being an annoying bastard" was perhaps a little vague, yet clearly suited to both his natural abilities and tendencies.

But what of the other Greatcoats? What of those asked to tread paths that led only to uncertainty and pain? What of those for whom the cost of devotion to the King's wishes would be higher than their hearts could bear?

There's a moment in Tyrant's Throne when Falcio is facing the thirteen rebel Greatcoats who've just returned to the fold after the near-fatal Scorn ride Chalmers undertook precisely because Falcio knew it would make the renegades realize how far they'd fallen. He looks at each of them, recalling how they'd first joined the King's Order of Travelling Magistrates. For a moment his eyes turn to Murielle de Vierre, the King's Thorn. We know what he saw in her: the beautiful woman he'd once trained and with whom he'd nearly begun a romantic relationship. But what did she see in Falcio's gaze? Was it loss and sorrow, or perhaps something darker that Falcio fails to recognize in himself: a brutal rejection of another for having failed to live up to the near-impossible standards to which he holds himself and everyone around him.

What would the consequences of that moment be for someone who had desperately wanted to be worthy of the mantle of Greatcoat but whose vision of themselves has been shattered into a thousand pieces? Where would she go next? What would the future hold for her?

I think Murielle de Vierre deserved better from Falcio. She certainly deserved better from the author who so casually put her upon the page only to dismiss her a few lines later. Let this tale serve as a first, tentative act of redemption, because I have a feeling the King's Thorn isn't the kind of person to settle for misery and disgrace for very long.

NOTES ON MEMORIES OF FLAME

The little boy whistled, and the fire grew.

This was the third Estevar Borros story I wrote, driven, I think, by the fact that I was enjoying his voice so much.

That's a funny term, "voice". When it comes to literature, we can't hear a character's timbre or pitch, whether their vocal tones are painfully nasal or so deep they make the floor rumble. What we do get are the things they choose to say and how they say them – along with something equally important: what they choose *not* to say.

I love writing Falcio val Mond because in many ways he's like an old film noir detective mixed with a Shakespearean tragic hero. He makes quips and snappy comebacks that sometimes expand into full-on speeches about idealism and injustice. He's always aiming for the most poignant word or sentence – the thing that will change the minds of those hardened by cynicism and despair.

Estevar isn't like that at all. At the precise moment when Falcio would launch into a speech, Estevar tends to become quiet. His interest is in the case before him, in the hidden truth and uncovering the workings of something supernatural. He'd much rather sit down to a good meal and let other people pontificate about the world, leaving Estevar to wonder when the next enigmatic occurance will come along for him to investigate.

And yet, a Greatcoat is a Greatcoat. Estevar can never fully distance himself from humanity and its concerns, nor can he ignore venality. He tries to let insults slide, yet when someone awakens the fire in him, then his rapier will surely be released from its scabbard. Woe be the opponent who underestimates Estevar Valejan Duerisi Borros' skill with a blade.

Speaking of fire, this story was never meant to be about fire. I began with the heat coming from the hearth in the cottage because I wanted Estevar to be physically uncomfortable and through that discomfort hide some of the spectral nature of the unfolding events. Once I started with that mention of flames, however, it carried through the scene and then into the crimes for which Olivier faced damnation from the priests. Whether I succeeded in keeping the ending from being predictable at the outset is up to the reader to decide, but for me, at least, Estevar, as he always does, provided a number of surprises along the way.

NOTES ON THE ASSASSIN'S HERESY

I like to remind myself sometimes that I'm not a murderer.

Disguise plays an interesting role in fantasy. It's exciting to witness, full of ingenious bits of makeup and clothing, almost like watching a theatre actor prepare to take the stage. But when reading those scenes, I often feel as if something's missing. Is it really all just a matter of fake beards and silly accents? Surely it takes more than this to embody someone else in a way that can be sustained and convincing.

When I was working on Our Lady of Blades and writing some of the scenes in which Lady Consequence constructs her disguises, I found myself far more curious about her internal transformation than the external trappings of fine dresses and luxuriant wigs. I began to wonder at the inner turmoil that must be enacted on someone as step by step they remove their sense of self to replace it with an identity that can never truly be theirs. It also occurred to me that by creating her internal disguise she was imbuing herself with the ability not only to behave as someone else, but also to contemplate acts that would otherwise be foreign to her nature.

But while Lady Consequence is many things, she's not a murderer. I wanted to explore the process by which a professional assassin in a world like Tristia might go about transforming themselves into the perfect lure for their intended victim. And as I wrote the story, I discovered something unexpected: my nameless assassin momentarily overcome by the allure of their own false persona and the possibility of an entirely different life. How, I asked myself, does someone like her resist that temptation? Then the second to last line came to me: *A murderer is an amateur who need kill only once. An assassin is a professional who must kill twice, and make of herself the first victim.*

It's a terribly dark thought, but then, killing is a pretty terrible business.

NOTES ON THE WHEELWRIGHT'S DUEL

In the first chapter of Saint's Blood, the third novel in my Greatcoats series, I open with a scene in which the reader is invited to imagine what it would be like to walk into their first duel: the herald coming to present you the writ confirming that you're required by law to fight a duel that day, stepping inside the duelling court, seeing for the first time the opponent who may well mean to kill you, and finally, having to take up the sword in the desperate hope that you might somehow win.

Of course, Saint's Blood is a story about Falcio val Mond, perhaps the greatest living duellist in Tristia (though Kest might disagree), so I never really answer the question of how in the names of all the Gods and Saints you're supposed to *win* that duel.

Trial by combat is, let's face it, a pretty cruel and brutal means of achieving justice. In our own world, it was rarely allowed because even our ancestors – who we always assume were more brutish than ourselves – considered it barbaric. Sensibilities of various historical eras either muted or amplified that perception, and people found all sorts of ways around laws forbidding duelling, but it was always a dubious pursuit.

Tristia is a different nation than any on our own world, however, with a richer and vastly more complex tradition of duelling and trial by combat. In my novel, Our Lady of Blades, I explore it in more detail than in the Greatcoats series, but even there I was dealing with an expert swordswoman facing other experts.

In this tale, I wanted to write about what it would be like to be someone swept up in a duelling trial, and who, being considered unimportant in the scheme of things, is about to become the victim of an entirely legal murder. Under Tristian duelling laws, a *duella verdetto* requires the magistrates to evenly match the opponents. However it's easy enough to sweep those distinctions under the rug, as the Magistrate does here by declaring that since neither Janva nor Praezan are professional duellists, and since the Gods – and the audience – like the idea of the brother of the victim rising to face her attacker, the two are well matched.

Often Greatcoats stories involve someone like Falcio or Kest swooping in to save the day. Here I wanted them to instead use the insight gained over countless duels to allow someone else to fight for themselves. I hadn't intended at first that Janva should consider becoming a Greatcoat herself, but by the time I came to the end of the story, it struck me that she might well make an excellent one.

That's the thing about duels: no matter how much you

think you know about the opponent, there's always a chance they might surprise you.

Oh, and a big thank you to sword expert Guy Windsor who kindly helped me work out some of the details of Janva's duel-ending maneuver!

NOTES ON DUEL WITH THE DEMON

Sparks erupted where the steel blades met, floating down to the loose hay covering the hall's stone floor.

There's a danger to opening lines. I spend a lot of time working on them – which itself is perilous because while I'm fretting over them I'm not writing the rest of the tale. But the real trap is that an opening line can veer you off from the direction you intended to go with your story in the first place.

Case in point, what became Duel with the Demon, the second Estevar Borros adventure, was meant to involve a woman coming at the end of a day of legal pleadings to introduce one more case: a suit against the mystical force possessing her daughter. Estevar's interests lean towards the supernatural, after all, and one of the reasons for writing him is to explore a side of Tristia that most other

Greatcoats – especially Falcio-I-Hate-Magic-val-Mond tend to ignore.

But when I picked that first line – and it's not even all that impressive a first line – I was suddenly stuck with this image of two swords slamming against each other so hard they shed sparks. Why had those swords struck? Who was holding them and why were they fighting so poorly?

I tried to dispense with the issue quickly so I could get on to some proper demon possession, but that damned line had set me down a path that had nothing to do with the supernatural, and instead forced Estevar to get out of his comfort zone and deal with some *real* evil – namely the kind human beings conjure up every day.

It took three passes to get the story to where I wanted it, but by the end, it seemed to me that Estevar had travelled down a more interesting road than I'd first intended and the King's Crucible would from now on take a greater interest in the mundane matters that affect so many people's lives in his troubled country.

Does that mean he's done with the supernatural? No more ghosts, spiritual interrogations, witchcraft investigations, and other ventures into matters maddening and mystical?

Knowing Estevar Valejan Duerisi Borros as I'm beginning to, I doubt that very much!

NOTES ON WHEN THE SWORD SEEMS TO SMILE

. . . and they lived happily ever after.

There's a phrase you stop buying into shortly after the third grade. This isn't cynicism, you understand; I'm a big believer in true love (having been the beneficiary of it for some time now). But once the dragon is slain and the wedding bells rung (hopefully not on the same day – that would be ghoulish), then comes the reality that relationships take work and traumas aren't shed as easily as old coats.

By my reckoning, Falcio has lived in a state of almost constant danger and bloodshed for nearly twenty years –

almost half his life. He's all too aware that there's a cost to violence – even violence committed in the defence of others. It's only natural that, as the physical dangers around him subside, the psychological ones he's kept buried (well, not that well buried – this is Falcio we're talking about here) would surface. How would such a person envision becoming a parent? Wouldn't they be terrified both of bringing the remnants of that violence with them into the family home *and* of the risk to their loved ones if the old defensive habits are set aside?

I've always liked that Ethalia is so different from Falcio. She's not morally or intellectually superior to him – just different. And it seemed to me that someone with her underlying compassion and sagacity would want to bridge the gap – not simply for her sake or for their child's sake, but for Falcio's as well. She would want to help him see himself as having something to offer his daughter beyond running off to beat up anyone who ever threatens her.

This story is about what's underneath Falcio's gift with a blade – the part that isn't about sticking the pointy end into the other guy first. It's about his impulse to attempt the impossible when the cause seems lost. It's about his underlying faith that friendship is a force more potent than any magic spell and stronger than any steel armour. Most of all, it's about a spirit of optimism and daring that infuses not only Falcio val Mond, but the stories of swash-buckling heroes that captivated me as a child and continue to do so today.

In fact, it's time I got back to writing a few more of

those stories myself. And so, with much affection and appreciation, I leave you now.

Sebastien de Castell
Vancouver, Canada
November 4th, 2021

OTHER BOOKS BY SEBASTIEN DE CASTELL

THE GREATCOATS SERIES

Traitor's Blade

Knight's Shadow

Saint's Blood

Tyrant's Throne

THE COURT OF SHADOWS SERIES

Our Lady of Blades

Play of Shadows

THE SPELLSLINGER SERIES

Spellslinger

Shadowblack

Charmcaster

Soulbinder

Queenslayer

Crownbreaker

Way of the Argosi

Fall of the Argosi

COLLECTIONS

Tales of the Greatcoats Vol. 1

SHORT FICTION ON DECASTELL.COM

A Study in Steel

Dance of the Chamberlain

Death of the Swashbuckler

Duel With the Demon

Memories of Flame

The Fox and the Bowman

The Obsidian Worm

The Red Lily

When the Sword Seems to Smile

... and more to come soon!

WANT MORE STORIES?

If you'd like an absolutely free short story from either my Spellslinger or Greatcoats fantasy series, drop by decastell.com and sign up to my mailing list for occasional updates, giveaways, and secrets about my books not published anywhere else. You can unsubscribe at the click of a button any time.

ABOUT THE AUTHOR

 Sebastien de Castell had just finished a degree in Archaeology when he started work on his first dig. Four hours later he realized how much he actually hated archaeology and left to pursue a very focused career as a musician, ombudsman, interaction designer, fight choreographer, teacher, project manager, actor, and product strategist. His only defence against the charge of unbridled dilettantism is that he genuinely likes doing these things and that, in one way or another, each of these fields plays a role in his writing. He sternly resists the accusation of being a Renaissance Man in the hopes that more people will label him that way.

Sebastien's acclaimed swashbuckling fantasy series, The Greatcoats. was shortlisted for both the 2014 Goodreads Choice Award for Best Fantasy. the Gemmell Morningstar Award for Best Debut, the Prix Imaginales for Best Foreign Work, and the John W. Campbell Award for Best New Writer. His YA fantasy series, Spellslinger, was nominated for the Carnegie Medal and is published in more than a dozen languages.

Sebastien lives in Vancouver, Canada with his lovely wife and two belligerent cats. You can reach him at www.decastell.com

Made in United States
Troutdale, OR
09/10/2023

12799558R00192